Breaking Hearts

Breaking Hearts
Simon Gray

faber and faber
LONDON · BOSTON

First published in 1997
by Faber and Faber Limited
3 Queen Square London WC1N 3AU

Typeset by Faber and Faber Ltd
Printed in England by Mackays of Chatham plc, Chatham, Kent

A CIP record for this book
is available from the British Library

ISBN 0–571–17238–5

2 4 6 8 10 9 7 5 3 1

For Victoria

I've no actual grounds for believing that my students refer to me as the waddler, or even think of me as the waddler. Why should they, apart from the fact that in fact I waddle? But my students are on the whole too dim to notice even my coarsest physical characteristics – the wart underneath my nose, the thickness of my neck, my slightly soiled blouse (it soils itself the moment I put it on, however clean my hands), my dumpling legs, my shoes that only *look* sensible, while actually gripping my swelling and throbbing feet. I would possibly be more comfortable in high-heels, spikey, clicking high-heels, red high-heels. Be more comfortable but look more preposterous. This bloated professor waddling in her red high-heels and crumpled garments through the hells of Academe. It would be as if I were in drag, passing myself off as feminine while all the world can see that (for identificational purposes, passport, etc.) I'm merely a woman, of no known sex.

I sometimes suspect that my office smells as strongly of gin as my study here at home, where I am now sitting. If sitting isn't too self-flattering a word to describe my posture. Completely immobile, I still waddle, my inert body waddling in a chair at its desk. Can the students smell the gin, is the question? Or is even the smell of physical decay too esoteric for university students these days?

Sissy now. Sissy. What does she do? I hear little snips and snaps of noise, feet scudding past my door; she's probably in her room, back from somewhere entertaining, on her way to somewhere exciting, with just enough time in between to rap through a phone call to Australia, at my expense. Everything she does in London is at my expense. No, no, I'm being unfair, and being unfair is not my strong suit. After all, though she's still a child (twenty-nine years and three months old), she does make occasional efforts on my behalf. For one thing she accompanies me to the opera. But then who buys the tickets? And where was she the night she failed to turn up for *Carmen*? I've never for a minute believed her story about not being able to get to a telephone to warn me that she'd be late. Or was it that her watch had 'malfunctioned', as she'd put it. Whichever story, taxi or watch, I don't believe it.

I sit for a while, sipping, smoking, smoking, sipping, thinking. Above me I can hear the scream of a jet soaring out of Heathrow. To Sydney. Or such places.

On the desk is a diary. It's been there for a week or so at least, and I haven't yet bothered to read it. The title page sports a jarring dedication to myself. 'For Dr Helena Twiscombe, PhD, from a grateful student. In Memoriam.' 'In Memoriam'? Which of us is 'in memoriam', the 'grateful' student or Dr Twiscombe, PhD? Nevertheless there are slight stirrings of professional guilt. I must have requested this work with some specific educational purpose in mind. But the 'in memoriam', to whichever of us it is meant to apply, has become an irritant. I reach out my hand, turn the heap on to its back, leaving me with merely a blank last page to disregard. I light another cigarette from the tip of the one I'm just finishing, swallow down another mouthful of gin.

There is someone on the other side of the door that isn't me. A rustling, a scent that slips through the reek of gin, nicotine and me that isn't mine.

I must get to a meeting. That's where I need to be. In my peer group. No, that's arrogance. They're not my peer group, they're in the most important respect my superiors.

Now, on my desk, there is a double heap of the 'grateful' student's blank diary. My eyes are full of tears. But why? What are they from? Not from loss. There's been no loss. Only the premonition of loss. With which I've become familiar since she arrived. Since before her arrival, to tell the truth. It must be the steady gulping down of bottled melancholia. My eyes go back to the two upside-down packs on the desk. The shadow of a third seems to be forming, up-side up, black blurs straggling across the page. If I pull the shadow to me, will it become substance, the words of my name written by the 'grateful' student, one of us 'in memoriam'. I reach out my hand, lower it through the shadow until it meets what should be there to be met.

What have I done to deserve this shame, when I have so much to be proud of? I'm not just a highly respected teacher but a writer. A writer of *books*. There they are on my shelves, the bulky three of them, my name on the spines, published by the Oxford University Press, or O.U.P. as we call it, those of us who are dignified by their request for our work. Three 'detailed and elegant, humane and learned' (*Times Literary Supplement*) tomes, all on the same subject. No, not 'subject', *man*. A *great* man. And a great *man*. And there are all his books on my shelves. His novels, his diaries, his letters – the whole body that contains the immense largeness of the soul of Charles Dickens. He lived in servitude. Servitude to his genius. Yes. His genius took him at an early age, five years younger than I am now, took him by his heart and brain, and drained him to his lees. You won't find this sort of stuff in my books, the stuff that makes me want to cry. I am, in fact, crying again. More splotches on my already splotched blouse.

I mustn't pour myself another gin. Light another cigarette. What I must and shall do is make a phone call, find out where the nearest meeting is. There's always one happening somewhere, thank God. I'll surge down the hall, and if Sissy's in, 'Ho, ho,' I'll declaim. 'Ho, ho, and damn. Got to go back to the College to pick up some papers I forgot. Outlines for tomorrow's seminars.' She won't know that I've been cancelling seminars and have already cancelled tomorrow's seminars. Then out on to the street, into a taxi. I'll give the address of the nearest meeting, then sit there trying not to look at the back of the cabbie's neck. Backs of necks are bad places to look at, especially when you suspect the driver knows the significance of the address, knows the meaning of the meeting. I shall maintain my dignity, nevertheless. Pass myself off for what I have been, and shall soon be again, and therefore still am: a formidable academic, a distinguished author, on my way to a conference. I shall speak at the meeting, for the very first time. I shall share the experience of what it's like to find myself chemically chained to disgusting substances, not the least of which is myself. It won't be a confession, merely a frank account of disgrace. It will be hard. Everything worthwhile is hard. But the people at the meeting are good people. They will hear the horrors of me and they will smile, lovingly, like adoptive parents. You are you, their smiles will say. Poor you.

There's only a last glass left in the last bottle. Gulp it down, make your phone call, off you go.

'Hello,' I shall begin. 'Hello,' I shall say. 'My name is Dr Helena Twiscombe, PhD!'

No, no, I can't say that. No last names, professional credentials attached. We're anonymous to each other. That's what makes it possible for us to be unashamed of our shame.

I've just seen what I thought was a face at the window, silhouetted in the darkness outside. I thought for a second it was Sissy, but then another silhouette formed opposite it. And behind, darker than the surrounding darkness, a waddling bulk, gathering in bulk as it waddled towards the profiles. The apparition lasted for a blink of an eye. For a blink of an eye I saw the two profiles connected, like sister and sister, lover and lover. The lump of darkness brought them together and enshrouded them.

Of course the bulk was the tree outside my window, waddled forward by a cloud crossing the moon. And of course the two profiles were merely leaves turned towards each other by the breeze. There is no tree outside. No cloud crosses the moon. I've just had an hallucination. That's all.

But why am I sitting here at my desk? Surely I came here to write an article on a matter of some significance. I've been writing something every evening, here at this desk in my study, year after year. But this evening there's only a ghostly memory of having written. Otherwise thoughts of Sissy to the screams of planes rising from Heathrow.

Teach me to care and not to care, teach me to sit still, if only for a moment.

'My name's Helena,' I shall say. 'I'm an alcoholic.' 'Hi and hello,' they'll comfort me. 'Hi and hello, Helena.'

I stand up, stumble slightly, steady myself by resting my hand on the 'grateful' student's diary which has reverted to a single heap. I turn it over to show it some respect. There they are again, the words. 'In memoriam'. I put the title page to one side, promising that when I come back I shall perform my teacher's duty. And there is the first sentence, unavoidable.

I stroked my calves, my thighs, half-dreaming of what lay ahead, of what I was going to do with Sissy, what I'd be doing to *you*, Twiskers, as I did it. I suddenly realized what I was in fact now doing to myself – no, no, not here, not in *this* bed! No wasting. So to a quick bowl of muesli with a banana in it, into the bathroom for all the usual, followed by a bath. The leather trousers, a green shirt, and of course the jeans jacket. I looked in the mirror, and there was the glowing, unblemished skin, the questing, innocent eyes. Nose, chin, etc. in mint condition. I stood back to take me in, the whole kit and caboodle of me. I would do. Yes, I would more than do. I was all of a piece. Harmonious, that's it. Harmonious.

'Teach me to care and not to care, teach me to have fun.'

On the tube nothing but the usual scum. Respectable scum going to their offices, banks, libraries, whatever

– unrespectable scum, no tickets, no hope, off to another station, another platform, another bench to lie on. Clutching their bottles of cider. If they're lucky, wine.

Change at Tottenham Court Road. Nip through the 'No Entry' hole into the Central Line. More debris roaming around, some with dogs. I hate them most. Dogs? 'Dogth ith wundeful critters, thquire!' You're always quoting that, from *Martin Chuzzle* . . . – no, *Hard Times*, that's it – always quoting it when you're describing the antics of some dog you owned in your childhood, Twiskers. If you had one. Childhood or dog. Whatever, the quote has somehow dribbled itself into my mind. Because they *are* wonderful creatures, dogs. And to see them carried about like, like orphans rented by gypsies – if you ask for money, you ask for yourself or for your professional orphan. Not on behalf of your wonderful dog. Shaming.

Tramp down the Mile End Road, feeling like a tramp. Keep up morale by turning myself into a harlot. Harlotting all the way down the Mile End Road and through the porticoes of the Dump. Joined by poor old Left-Overs. His nickname among the students is Scruff, but to me he's a Left-Overs. He's touching fifty, has greying brown hair almost to his shoulders, a Jesus beard, and the one time I went to his flat he played Beatles tunes on his guitar, smoked a joint which I wouldn't share with him – 'What's the matter? Uptight?' he said with a kind of loose and hopeless sneer. 'Uptight' I swear he said, and for supper there was a bottle of Chianti with which I couldn't wash down the spaghetti bolognese, and then there was the gentle attachment of his hand to my knee, and then the gentle detachment when I enquired after the subjects of all the photos everywhere you looked.

'Children, grandchildren, what?'

'They huppen to be nieces, naivews, goochildrrrun.'

He tries to keep his Scots accent in good working order.

'Not married at the moment, then?'

'Naiver bin married.' The r's in 'married' went on and on and on. 'Och, I've had a laife. Varrrious life.' Back came the hand. Off went the hand. And the accent. That went off too.

Ended in tears. Confessions. Right down the small damp tunnel – no, dank. Down the small *dank* tunnel of his life we trudged together. Some of the tears were mine, but I was crying from the boredom of it, the depression. God, why can't people, men and women, be single with dignity? Well then, without self-pity. Well then, without drenching you with their self-pity. Fucking self-pity. And the fucking Beatles. And he wasn't even drunk.

Why do I hate them so much, the Beatles? Those old pictures of the smirking moppets – especially the one who was gunned down outside his apartment block. Lennon. With his Jap wife. Lying about in the nude, in shop windows and stuff. I could kill the guy who shot him, for all the rubbish and crap he let loose on the world. Vigils in parks, those granny specs – that's Left-Overs too. Granny specs, long hair, his Jesus chin, a joint, the Chianti, the spaghetti, the hand on my knee again.

'Are you by any chance *queer*?' I asked him, swatting his hand away.

'Gay, don't you mean?'

'Whatever. Are you?'

'Whut I am,' he said, 'Is sexyoual.'

'But never married,' says I, with a crisp smile. Like a shrink, really.

'Too busy living.' He says this sucking on his joint. 'But there've been – been some daiths, you know.' That's when the tears began.

'Have you got an allergy?' Very innocent and sympathetic, the way I put it to him. My own eyes dry, pouting my lips.

'Whut?'

'Well, something's made your eyes go red and watery.'

'Chrrrist!' he said. 'I didn't know – I didn't know there were people like you!'

'There aren't people like me. Just me. And just me doesn't like people like you putting a hand on a knee.'

Outside, on the pavement, I looked up at his window. His Jesus chin jutted soulfully towards me, his hand raised in forgiveness. Or pleading? But pleading for what? A fuck and some cuddles. That's what.

Well, why not? I'll tell me why not. For one thing there's Aids, isn't there? Types like Left-Overs, who have been left all over the place for two and a half decades, with their 'sexyouality'. One little cut! No thanks!

The funny thing is that since that evening we've been all right, Left-Overs and me. Not quite pals or muckers or mates or friends even. But there's been more than just peaceful co-existence between us.

He knows I'm tough. Much tougher than he is. He says I'm one of the few – once he said the *only*, but that's a left-over's lie – the *only* one from his seminars

9

who's said no. This year there are eight in his seminar, and I know for a fact that he's picked off at least five. Five! And they're proud of it! They mostly adore him, think his sex-and-pot sessions are a privilege, and the next morning, you can always spot which one he's had, he or she is so silly-pleased, smiling to him or her self.

Being a left-over, he likes us, actually likes us, to read the plays and the sonnets and try to understand what the lines mean, what the characters are like, what the feelings are about, how the drama works. All the stuff that's interesting. Just like you, Twiskers, I'll give you that. Give him that too. Unlike a lot of the rest of the lecturers, etc., who probably can't read a line of Shakespeare. Understand it, anyway. We've got feminist courses, gay courses, black courses, feminist gay black courses, all the structuralist, de-constructuralist, historicist, all that. So Left-Overs is a relief. Of course he's got his own special left-over speciality going on. He gets excited over mystical crap, particular numbers and anagrams turning up all over the place, in monologues in J. Caesar, Corio, Meas for Meas, and there's one example in Sonnet 46, is it? where the rhyme scheme – what am I doing, what am I going into this for? I've already written five essays at the last count on Left-Overs' crap. I take it all in, swallow it down, with the intention of throwing it all up again, because he's always – *always* – on the Board of Examiners, and he'll know, acknowledge, and mark highly his own crap when he smells it coming off the page back at him. Coprophiliac, that's the word for him, isn't it? An intellectual coprophiliac when it comes to mystics and numbers and anagrams. But

10

apart from being a coprophiliac he's not a bad teacher. As I say. Fair's fair.

So there he was, and there was me. I. There was I. Going up the steps into the mean hallway of the Dump. He was wearing shades instead of the grannies because he had a hangover. There were flecks of this and that on and in the Jesus chin, milk and dead yoghurt. Nescafé dribblings.

'Look,' he said, 'I've been thinking. Time to sort out the production.' (I'm fucked if I'm going to do all his r's any more. Boring. Take them as read, Twis. You know him as well as I do.) 'Do you want to be in it?'

'Oh, I don't know,' I said. 'An amateur production. And in the Dump.'

'Well, you have to start somewhere. And you'd glitter. I'd make sure you got a glittering something, I promise. It's *Romeo and Juliet*.

'Romeo *and* Juliet. Now you're talking. Yes, I can handle those.'

He laughed.

'I'm serious,' I said. 'I'm only interested if I do both.'

'What, on the same night?'

'No, no, I'll alternate. All you've got to do is line up a decent Romeo for my Juliet, and a decent Juliet for my Romeo.'

'And how will you play them? *Your* Romeo and *your* Juliet?'

'Look at me. Look at me and imagine.'

He looked at me. He imagined.

When we reached the staff room, he took his shades off, stuck them in his pocket, popped on his grannies. He strummed his fingers through his Jesus, rearranging the blobs and patches of his breakfast into more

11

inconspicuous sites, and peered through the open doors to where his academic colleagues sat at their little tables on their little chairs, which gave some of them the look of pension-orientated and useless elves. They sipped at their coffees and teas, nibbled at their biscuits, as if they'd come on from a funeral for a brother elf they didn't particularly like.

'You can't come in here,' Left-Overs said firmly.

'Why not? We had coffee last week.'

'Yes. Because I invited you. But now I'm not inviting you. So you can't come in.'

'OK.'

'See you at the auditions, Romeo. And you too, Juliet.'

We laughed. A proper laugh. Do I want it? Get fond of people and – ? Therefore. Yes, therefore –

'Therefore.' I caught his sleeve.

'Therefore what?'

'Therefore I'm coming in for coffee.'

'Like hell you are. I told you to fuck off. Fuck off therefore.'

I bounded past him to the counter. There she was, a miserable creature, with small, malevolent brown eyes, a mouth like a rat's, two teeth protruding and no visible lips.

'Coffee,' I said urgently.

'Are you a member of the staff?'

'Good morning, Mrs H.' Left-Overs had re-institutionalized himself in a matter of seconds, simultaneously *de haut en bas* – in one of your phrases, Tee-Hee, PhD – and 'grovelling', in one of *my* phrases, Twigs.

'Would you explain to this woman exactly who I am?'

'No, I won't. Who are you?'

'I'm with you and I want a cup of coffee.'

A trifling silence. Mrs H.'s small brownies sparkled with filthy hopes.

Left-Overs broke. I knew he would. He hated himself for it. And hated me for it.

'A student of mine,' he said. 'Entitled to coffee, Mrs H. We were just horsing around, eh?' His eyes dodged all over the Staff Common Room – green carpet, dead and bloated elves lolling in their plastic-backed cups of chairs, great lumps of shiny paint sticking out of frames on the walls. There was one that looked like a turd on an aquamarine table, called 'Hong Kong Harbour: Dawn', so perhaps it was a giant turd floating in Hong Kong Harbour, at dawn. There was also one that looked like a foetus in a sombrero, called 'Kowloon Peasant'. And there was another – I can't be bothered, and anyway Left-Overs wasn't looking at the pictures, he was clocking the dead elves.

'There's the effing Dean,' he muttered, as Mrs H. turned her rounded shoulders on us, and poured the coffee. He nodded his head towards the Staff Common Room's senior dead elf, who was togged out in his usual grey suit, a briefcase at his feet.

'Where's the effing Dean?' I squealed excitedly. 'You mean the effing Dean's actually here, in this very room. This very, very common room and there's the effing Dean in it!'

The effing Dean, getting all this, went into incredulous focus.

Mrs H. juddered around with the coffee, which she shared impartially between cup and saucer. The rat-teeth and brownies pointed at Left-Overs.

'I don't like swearing at my counter. Especially with the Dean,' she said loudly.

Well, of course, some things you're entitled not to resist.

'What were you swearing at it for?' I asked eagerly.

'What?'

'What were you and the effing Dean swearing at the counter for? And how do you do it? Do you stand opposite each other, I mean, or does he come and stand beside you' – my voice was full-pitch, but sort of natural, I think – 'and swear away together? At the counter? And why?'

Left-Overs grabbed at the coffee. His hands, trembling, helped some more black acid from the cup into the saucer, and some from the saucer on to his shoes. The supreme dead elf was wincing his eyes and furrowing his brow.

'Why are you doing this?' Left-Overs went to the furthest table, in a corner, under a picture of a purple person standing in a field of yellow corn, it looked like, until you glimpsed the title, which was 'A Cantonese Banquet. Still Life'.

I wasn't having it. 'I'm not sitting under that! There's a table right here.' And hunkered gracefully down at the table next to the dead elf supreme, currently known as the effing Dean. Whose eyes wilted away from me. He crouched down, picked up his briefcase, pulled out some papers.

Left-Overs came over, sat down. I'd spun a nightmare around him, all right. That's how he sat down, if you see what I mean.

'Morning, Jeff,' he said, with lots of bobs of head and even wringing of hands. Uriah Heaping away at his effing Dean, while trying to give me homicidally controlling looks. 'Morning, Jeff,' he said again, louder, more desperate.

'Morning, Foster.'

'Tell us again about the other night you told us about the other day.' From me, of course.

'What?' This was a kind of menacing yelp from Left-Overs.

'Because I didn't know people in your position could get away with that sort of thing.'

Effing Dean, whose whole job is meant to be about this sort of thing, had turned himself back into dead elf.

'What are you talking about?' What a clown, Left-Overs. Instead of changing a subject which could lead to his dismissal, even a court case and jail, he actually invited me to enlarge on it. Which I did.

'Your troilism. Isn't that what it's called? Troilism?' I made it sound like a form of tobogganing.

The dead elves stopped moving their lips and nodding their heads. All those writhing still-lifes became as still as death.

I wondered which way he'd go. Would he roll his rrrr's until he'd recovered his wits, or would he shriek straight into it.

'You're talking absolute rubbish –' he shrieked. Jolly nearly 'wubbish' it came out as, no r's or Scots of any kind. 'Wubbish. Misunderstood evwything. There wasn't a bed. Just a – a – an informal seminar. On my own time. With excellent students of both sexes, and now – now –'

He went A.W.O.L. for a good, for him bad, ten seconds.

'– now I've got a class.' Our eyes met and just for a flash, through his grannies, I saw disaster. He made a choking noise, scratched meaninglessly at his Jesus, strode out of the morgue.

I was therefore alone to work over the supreme dead, who went on snuffling into his papers. I made mewling sounds, like a deranged kitten.

'Pardon?' he asked at last, putting his papers down. Yes, that's what he said, the Dean of Arts, he said 'Pardon?' Why not the whole hog – 'Pardon me, I have to go to the toilet, could you pass me a serviette as sometimes they run out of toilet –'

'Pardon?' he said again with a hapless, hopeless, helpless gesture, which ended in his knocking his coffee cup over.

'Blast, blast, blast!' He really wanted to say what any red-blooded effing would want to say in the circumstances, which would be 'Fuck, fuck, fuck! Oh God, how I'd love to fuck you!' Because I have this effect, you see. Not only on 'human beans' and dead elves and effings, but on virtually all creatures great and small. Don't believe me, but there was a parrot once, belonged (probably still does; it was only in its late forties when I knew it) to parents of a friend of mine, and every time I went around this parrot gave me the eye. I could see *it* in the eye it was giving me. All it could gutteral out was 'You OK, you OK, you OK.' Its name was Henry and it sat in its cage, its eye absolutely on me, trying to get this needy eye into my eye, and then into my brain and then down between my legs.

So when cats plop into my lap. When dogs jump and sniff.

When people, all those people, and all *these* people give me the eye, between-my-legs (let's shorten this to b.t.l. – not to be confused with b.l.t., which is a sandwich, Twiskers) – b.t.l. is always aware. Because b.t.l. is right in the centre of my brain.

'Please,' I said, 'please be so kind – so kind –'

'Yes?' he said. 'Yes?' He reached towards me.

'If you wouldn't mind –'

'Yes? Yes?'

'Not touching me. I've had too much touching from people. Here. In your college, sir.'

His hand fell like a wounded whatever you like to earth. Which was his lap. 'If there's anything the College can do. We've got people. People you can talk to. Mmm?'

I got up, turned dramatically, pathetically, and a touch saucily – *not* an impossible combination, is it, Twiskers, if you've got a figure like mine – I mean, my *buttocks*! Shapely, tightly muscled mounds – and my legs, long, tapering – everything about the lower half of me I can make disturbing almost at will. Upper half, too.

Deansy-Weansy Beansy-Weansy Weansy-Deansy or Bunsy-Wunsy, whoever, stared into some exotic future in which he saw Left-Overs behind bars, while he himself committed elfish offences against my person.

I romped through the tatty corridors of the Dump, nudging the drab students of both sexes out of the way but giving them gloriously radiant smiles, smiles that lit up their bleak days and for a second or two demeaned – no. That's not the word. I'll have to think on this one. Diminished. Yes. That's it. Diminished for a second or two their sense of uselessness, purpose-lessness, futurelessness in this world of theirs.

First a quick spot-check on the Dump's Student Common Room. No Sissy. Of course not. Although she's always the first person I look for, even though I know she isn't there. What I have to do is find out where she is, and that's up to you, isn't it, Twiscombe, PhDrunkard? What there was was about a dozen students (that looks terrible, 'was was', but to hell with it!), sitting in groups of two or three. *But* at least *and* thank God, Herman and Sylvester. The only students with whom I permit myself to have dealings. They were sitting with Joey. Joey is one of the Americans the Dump's compelled to take to make ends meet. Her idea is to cut a swathe as a cute American boy, small, slender, all smiles, little twitches of the shoulder. The sort of thirteen-year-old you'd want to be when you're fifty. She's about twenty.

Herman is fat. So is Sylvester. Two cheerful chubbies, they hang out together, have the same haircuts, speak in the same nasal Jewish accents, and wear similar gear. Baggy jeans, suede jackets, thick blue shirts, trainers. Tweedle-dum and Tweedle-dum. They like reading, talking to each other and to everybody else about what they read – anachritisms. Wait a minute, PhDrinker, I'm going to check this out. Anachronisms. They're anachronisms. They're not even related but the only difference between them is that Sylvester damaged a knee running, then toppling, then crashing down the stairs when he was six. This knee, his left (or right, depending), he rubs a lot, massaging it and grimacing. Apparently it itches almost all the time, but he can never *find* the itch, with his fingers. He wasn't massaging it now. He sat with his arms folded across his chest. As did Herman.

'I got this awful feeling,' Joey squeaked. (No, unfair. She doesn't actually squeak. It's a nice sound. But thin.

Let's think here. It's a gushy, innocent, girlish noise, a bit thin on the ear but richer than a squeak.) 'I got this awful feeling that something real bad was going to happen, and on the chube this morning this old lady with a dog and a lot of bags, she let this dog, it was a small mongrel sort of dog, it got off her lap and came over to me and licked at my hand and I stroked its head and then it went back and yapped. And the old lady, she was filthy, she said the dog, this dog, wanted to get paid, and I said, paid for what, and she said, licking your hand and yapping, it's a performing dog and gets paid, and this dog was yapping away, and this old lady, she got up and stood over me, and everybody watching. I mean, that's worse than the New York subway – oh, hi! I didn't see you there.'

I'd settled in between Herman and Sylvester.

'Ho,' said Herman.

'Ho,' from Sylvester.

'I was just telling Herman and Sylvester –'

'I know. I heard it. Go on. Do go on.' I did some cutes back at her, English style. Being American, she never understands anything about anything.

'And I said no, I can't give you any money, I don't have any money and she said something to the dog and the dog went down on me.'

'Went down on you?' This from Herman.

Sylvester: 'That's not date-rape. That's *rape*! The real thing!'

'What?' from Joey. 'It bit me! Look!'

She showed some little red nicks on her wrists.

'Oh, God!' I stared at the nicks, horrified.

Sylvester rubbed his knee. A sign, possibly, that he knew something was up.

19

Joey did some head and shoulder business. 'I mean, she's trained it to bite people who don't give her any dosh.' She's very proud of her little Englishisms, though actually she pronounced it 'dash'. Or perhaps she'd confused the two.

'Where? Where?' My voice was full of panic.

'On the chube. I told you.'

'Yes, but which line, which *line*? Not the Baker*loo*!' I guessed it, as she lives around Baker Street with friends of cousins, or something.

'Well, yes, Bakerloo, that's right. Why?'

'And it was an old woman and a small mongrel?'

Sylvester and Herman were clueing in. They're very quick like that. 'Oh dear God, the Bakerloo line,' said Herman, perfectly anxious.

'Isn't that the line – ?' from Sylvester.

'Now listen, Joey,' I said, 'I'm going to tell you something very important, and you've got to listen and keep very, very calm. All right?'

'What, what, what – ?' Her little face was white, her voice was Minnie Mouse.

'It's not too late,' I said. 'Herman, hold her hand.'

'I'll do it,' Sylvester said, and slipped his hand around her wrist.

'Herman, I think you should take the other one,' I said, absolutely in control in a situation of otherwise uncontrollable horror.

They sat there, Herman and Sylvester, holding the wrists of the cutesy. They looked enchanting in their bliss of squeezing her wrists.

'The thing is, Joey –' I took a deep breath. She was fixed on me in naked dread – yes, *naked* dread, and so of course for once, all her cuteness stripped away, I thought she was pretty cute. And cutely pretty. I could imagine belting and chaining *her*, in her naked dread. 'No way!' as she says quite often, 'No way!' would I want her dribble.

'– the thing is that a friend of mine works in Charing Cross Hospital and in the last week they've had – oh, Christ, they're such *fuckwits* these people!'

She longed to scream. 'You're not talking – not talking – here in England where they boast – you're not – oh, no, oh, no – you're not.'

'They think the dog was smuggled in, isn't that the rumour?' Herman said.

'The one I've heard, anyway. But not by her, of course. The old woman –' Sylvester was deep into his knee, with his free hand, as a way of keeping the joy off his face. He has a love of details, has Sylvester, as is shown in the essays he reads out in seminars.

Herman picked up on cue. 'The old lady adopted it. She's a tramp. They work the Bakerloo line.'

'But they're not sure!'

'The common factor in the cases –' from Herman.

'– is a bite from a dog owned by an old lady –' from Sylvester, scratching, scratching –

'– on the Bakerloo line.'

'Oh, shit. Oh, shit. Oh, shit!' Think of Minnie Mouse squeaking 'Oh, shit!' It was like that.

'But you know, there is the injection.' From Herman.

'It may be dreadfully painful –' from Sylvester.

'But a high-per-cent success rate.'

'I've got to! I've got to!' She got up. Herman and Sylvester, clamped to her wrists, rose with her.

'Which hospital? Which – ?'

The scattered tables were riveted on our American

cutie-pie, now having hysterics.

Having gone so far I didn't know whether I wanted to go further. Nor did Herman. Nor did Sylvester. They'd have been quite happy holding her between them for another minute or so, and then off to our seminar.

'This country! This shit of a country – !' she squeaked, everything going. That's what did it. She was a goner from those squeaks on.

I made the decision for us. 'Charing Cross,' I said briskly. 'Come with me.' I held out my hand. She wrenched herself free from Herman and Sylvester and put a hand into mine. I led her through the Common Room like some honest and terrified virgin. No. That makes *me* the honest and terrified virgin, grammatically. *She* was like an honest and terrified virgin. *I* was like a compassionate, considerate, caring, concerned – *all* the filthy 'c' words – but with something sexual added. I led my stricken little captive who'd just made an incomprehensible but emotional scene –

She stumbled after me. 'Where are we going?' she squeaked. 'I mean, how are we – how are we going to –?'

'You mustn't, please, dribble over me. You see, it's there. In the dribble. The negro bodies, I think they're called. And you're crying a bit. And dribbling. Are you thirsty? That's a sign. Thirsty and dread of water.'

'No – no – but where are we –?' I'd got her past the porter's desk, out through the doors, into what was called the forecourt.

A taxi drew up. A professor, from the look of him, got out of it. Thin, intense, middle-aged, sleek briefcase, mobile phone sticking out of his pocket. He was holding a twenty-pound note. I jerked Joey towards him.

'Six pounds fifty, take fifty p. for yourself.'

The note changed hands as I bowled past him, prodded Joey into the cab. 'Charing Cross Hospital, Out-patients,' I said urgently. 'I'm sorry, I can't come with you.'

'What's going on?' from the prof. Nice voice. Irish accent.

'Excuse me, sir,' I shouted over at him. 'This is a student. She's very ill. Needs immediate medical –' Then to Joey. 'Go to Out-patients. They'll see to you within an hour or two. Be patient!'

'Oh, this shit – this shit of a country!' she was sobbing. Her nose was running.

'My change,' said the prof. 'I've given you a twenty –'

'Please move,' I said to the driver, slamming the door on Joey. 'It's an emergency.'

'My change – I gave you a twenty and –'

The driver gunned off, thirteen pounds to the good. The prof stood facing me in the fore-dump, thirteen pounds to the bad.

'What the –' he was about to swear. Thought about the situation, Deansy-Weansy, students' union, tabloids, etc.

'She thinks she's rabid,' I explained.

His eyebrows, bushy and sandy, did a little jump. 'Really? And why should she think she's a rabbit?'

'*Rabid*. She claims she was bitten by an old woman. On the tube. And now she's on the verge of biting other people. She tried to bite me. She's American.'

'American,' he nodded, as if this was the major part of the explanation.

'Anyway, that's why I didn't go with her in the taxi. If she started yapping and biting at me, I'd be trapped.'

He looked at me, suddenly laughed. 'You're having me on!'

'No, I'm not, sir. She really does believe she's rabid.'

'Oh, bugger! I'll have to do something about her, won't I? What's her name?'

I told him.

'Well, she'll obviously have to be shipped home. Probably in a strait-jacket, eh?'

Something stirred b.t.l. at the thought of cutey-pie in a strait-jacket, on an airplane. The shame of it! But she shouldn't have said 'shit of a country'. *We* can say it, but they can't. At least while they're here. If they do they can expect to be treated like shit. A cute little shit in a strait-jacket is exactly what she deserved to be.

'And what's your name?'

'Oh gosh, what's the time, please, sir?'

'Five past eleven, are you the only student left in the U.K. who "sirs" the staff?'

'*Five past eleven*. I've got to dash. There's a seminar and I'll be in trouble.' I scrambled towards the steps.

'Your name?' I could hear him coming after me.

I jabbered out a confusion of consonants and syllables, got through the door, down the corridors. I wondered if I might find out about him, even let him have my name. The Irish accent. The sandy eyebrows. The laugh. Somebody to talk to when in trouble. So I might get him into trouble and talk to him. Hear *his* side of trouble.

Horatia, otherwise known as the Corrector, is black, fat and jolly. A real Aunt Jemima. So alive. I've often thought and hoped that instead of the thin, bespectacled white sociologist she turns up with at the Dump's functions called Esmé (yeah, yeah, a screwed-up sentence, Twiskers, but let's leave it, eh?) – what I've often hoped and thought is that Esmé, scrawny and grim and against everything white except herself, that Esmé is the Corrector's beard, and that every evening the Corrector goes home to a rollicking house run with a rod of velvet by a huge Jamaican lay-about – mainly laying about the Corrector with his rod of velvet, 'as a consequence of which', as Twiskunt would say – wouldn't you, old soak? – the house is swarming with children, and at night the whole family gets together and drinks a toast in rum to the imbecile whiteys, who *pay* her to abuse their male heterosexuals in seminars. *That* would be OK! *That* would be great!

But alas and alack, the poor fat Corrector only has her scrawny Esmé to go home to. And what do they do? What do they do together? Does the plump Corrector frolic with the scrawny body and its dead mind? Does the scrawny mind in the dead body frolic with the rollicking Corrector?

I opened the door. The Corrector stopped some lively heaving and chortling and gave me one of her humorously corrective looks. They're lethal. All that life. All that death. Both on offer.

'I'm sorry,' I whispered. 'Sorry. Joey went very sick. I had to get her to hospital.'

'Joey? What's her problem?' That's one of the Corrector's phrases, though she always makes it fat with compassion.

I explained at some length, sticking pretty well to the version I'd given to the prof in the fore-park, in case they exchanged notes in the Common Room.

Herman and Sylvester kept ducking their heads, trying to stay out of it, trying not to laugh.

'She tried to bite Herman, didn't she, Herman?'

Herman went into spastic movement. 'Not exactly a bite. And she did apologize.'

'Was it you, Sylvester,' I asked, 'she actually bit?'

'I'd rather not say, rather not say.' He began cuffing and beating his knee, to raise up the pain and block the laugh.

'Well, I just hope,' the Corrector said, 'that she comes through this,' (that's right, Twiskers, 'through this') 'and is back here with us soon. Mental illness is an ill-ness of the mind.'

Did she think we thought it was an illness of the feet, or a bout of piles?

'I don't think she'll be back with us soon, I'm afraid,' I said. 'You see, a professor, medical or legal, I don't know, but he saw her in the fore-play –'

'Where?'

'In the forecourt, I mean, and she, well, she kind of attacked him out of the way and clambered into his taxi, and he, well, he said that he would see to it that she'd be packed back to the States in a strait-jacket.'

All the jolly and compassionate rolls and heaves and twinkles stopped. She sniffed a campaign here.

'He said that, did he?'

'Like all the bloody Americans ought to be, he said. Anyway, he's going to report her. And get her deported. In a strait-jacket.'

The Corrector shed a lot of pounds and colour, in the sense that there was Esmé peering out of her.

'If he reports her he'll have to give *his* name too, won't he?' she said. I didn't answer, taking it to be a rhetorical. 'And then we'll see who ends up where.'

'He seemed very nice,' I said, with absolute truth.

'They – all – seem – very – nice!'

'What *they*?' I asked, with real, intense, learning-about-the-bigotry-from-any-source eagerness.

She was too smart for this. Or so she thought. 'Racists. Of any race.'

'No, I don't understand. I mean Joey's a white American, and this professor is a white Irishman. I don't understand how, well, the racial bit comes into this. For once.'

'What about the master-race and the servant-race? What about the teacher-race and the student-race?'

'I *see*!' I said. 'Yes, I see. But – but –'

Herman and Sylvester said almost together, under their breaths, 'Will you shut up!' and 'Cut it out, cut it out, cut it out!'

But Ms Piggy, one of the sickos (as in sycophants), loved the implications. She's short, fat, bespectacled *and* she smells. She's such a repulsive cartoon of the male idea of the aggressive feminist that I sometimes believe she's a double agent, paid huge sums by males to discredit the cause she pretends to espouse. I mean these days feminists have soft voices, frilly skirts, pleasing smiles. The ones I see on television anyway. They're *feminine* feminists, good to look at, good to listen to, there isn't a single one of the top ones I wouldn't want to see locked into a chastity belt, hands cuffed, neck collared, being led by a lead into the debating chamber or a television studio.

Anyway, one of the sickos – no, I've got beyond that to Ms Piggy, whom I definitely would not want to see naked, and don't like looking at even dressed or covered. She doesn't *dress*, but she does cover herself. In wads of clothing.

Sicko Ms Piggy said, 'That's the Marxist underpinning to feminism, isn't it, Horatia?'

Horatia the Corrector went straight into it for ten minutes, then five minutes of how previously received education, the famous great texts, were now to be seen in Marxist terms as the imprisoning of the working classes by the middle classes, and how values received from Charles Dickens, for instance –

'For instance'? Charlie D. a 'for instance'!

And then she *really* got going. Charlie D. 'for instance' is her special favourite hate. She starts with the marriage, his marrying one sister and then falling in love with the younger one, moving her into his ménage, where he adored, adored, *adored* her, and there was poor Catherine, the wife, the third party, watching this male monster of heterosexuality worshipping her little sister while being bored and irritated by herself, his actual wife, whose only fault, *only fault* was that she was clumsy, fell over things, was pretty stupid and couldn't speak coherently in public (in other words, a shame and a disgrace of a wife). And then the younger sister collapsing, dying, and Charlie D. making a meal of it, sobbing, making memorials and monuments to her, and Catherine, the wife, can you imagine? rolled and jollied the Corrector, what it was like to be Catherine, the wife, with this husband who insulted her by grieving over her dead sister, while at the same time she herself was producing children, some of them corpses!

'They made love then?' I ruminated to myself, but audibly. Bait, really. Up to her.

'Made?' she held up a pinkish palm. 'Love? He led his successful days, triumphant days, *famous* days, and then climbed into bed at night, straddled her and *fucked*

28

her. She had no say in this matter. No say.'

I looked and sounded shocked, I hope. 'You mean she didn't *ask* for it?'

The merry eyes went into reptilian Esmé-mode. 'Ask for it? She wasn't consulted. Not even consulted.'

'Consulted about whether she wanted sex?'

Herman and Sylvester were at it again. Shoulders on the heave.

The Corrector, who's not stupid about anything except the books she teaches –

'You two men, gentlemen,' she was quite flirtatious, 'you gentlemen find this funny, I think.'

Sylvester slapped his knee, for helpful pain. 'No, Horatia,' he said. 'It's a nightmare. Must have been a complete nightmare.'

'Yes,' I said earnestly, 'I mean, this poor, hopeless, clumsy, useless woman –'

'Useless?' Horatia, reptilian and Esméian.

'Rendered useless,' I said throbbingly.

'Ah yes. You see the point.' The reptilian went towards Herman, who was compelled to sit sideways, from suppressed hilarity. Unlike Sylvester, he had no easy means of causing himself pain, though his present predicament was pain in itself.

'Herman. Do *you* see the point?'

'Oh yes, yes, yes, I do!' And out it *almost* came, the shriek of laughter. 'Useless, hopeless – his fault. And still he wanted to – to – straddle and – and –'

'Fuck her,' Horatia filled in for him. 'Don't be afraid of the word, Herman.'

'I'm not, Horatia – fuck her! Aaaah! Feeling nauseous. Got to – got to –' he heaved himself off the chair. Out of the room. Howling.

Sylvester, of course, saw his chance. 'I'd better –' he said, pounding his knee as he rose, 'I'd better see that he's all right.' And he was out of the room.

Horatia was deeply suspicious. The thing about fought-against mirth is that it's there, in the atmosphere, electric and embarrassing, even if not identified as mirth.

She decided to ignore everything, launching a further assault on that genius of the ages, Charlie D. And I thought of Charlie D. meeting up with the Corrector, his eyes taking her in as he listened to her chortling voice, almost singing now she was, calypsoing out her imbecilities and dead ideas. God, what fun he would have had with her. And her Esmé. 'Charlie D., Charlie D.,' I yearned, 'come and look at this lot.'

Ms Piggy and the other sickos sat, like magistrates, heads tick-tocking out every charge against Charlie D. The rest sat mutely through it because the Corrector's course is an easy option. I mean, anyone knows how to answer the Corrector's exam papers, just peddle the simplest line, which you repeat over and over in slightly, but not extremely, different words.

I let her come to the end. She did what she always does. Looked around at all the faces in roly triumph and, yes, modesty.

'Thank you, Horatia,' said the sicko sitting next to Ms Piggy. She's infuriating. Her name is Sally Dean, and she's got pimples, wears soiled jeans, grubby ankles showing above her plimsolls. Real, old, old-fashioned plimsolls, the kind her mother used to wear, one of them had the laces undone. Always undone. And of course a turtle-neck sweater. Perhaps she dresses completely out of her mother's wardrobe. Or Oxfam. Yes –

that's it. She dresses from Oxfam, and provides the pimples herself. With no effort. She simply doesn't wash.

But she's infuriating because she's pretty, Twiskers, as you've probably noticed. Neat, tall body and pointy breasts. (Is she still into bra burning? Or are there no bras for sale in Oxfam?) Jutty buttocks. If you look at structure and form, bone structure that is, and the form of the head, oval-shaped, and close out the details, the spots and blackheads, the greasy black hair that could be shampooed into luxuriousness –

Well, if you can get to all she could be without throwing up because you're looking at what she is –

You could strap the belts and chains around her, spread-eagle her on a bed with the gag – you wouldn't want to hear her speak until you'd gagged the old-style feminist whine out of her – and sit beside her – oh, God, don't forget having washed and washed and washed her, had a brutal handmaiden pop the pimples, etc., lots of oils and lotions, trim the pubic hair, hold her down in the bath for two hours – then – then –

It's no good. What I really want to do with Sally Dean is *not* honour her with chains and padlocks, not Sissify and dignify her with ornaments of restraint and love, but stuff her into a rubbish bag.

'Thank you, 'Oratia,' she said. 'You move me, you know. I mean, I mean, this is meant to be a literary class, but here I am, touched and moved in my sexual.'

She said those very words, I swear, Twiskers. They're here on my pad. I wrote them down as she spoke.

'And thank you, Sally,' I said. 'You've just said something that helps me to, well, to understand the value of Horatia's course.' And I rapped this same pad with my filter-pen. 'The only thing that worries me,' I wondered if I ought to get up, fall to the floor in self-disgust. 'What worries me, you see, is this thing.'

'What thing?'

'This thing. It worries me. This thing of *me*, you see.' I did stand.

She was all urgent, caring, concerned, compassionate – all the 'c' words with comforting, Aunt-Jemima-rolling-of-the-flesh, to boot. Which I was about to.

'I don't understand.'

'Well. I mean. Like. Like. You get in this seminar, this seminar of yours, a student who – who –'

'A student who *what*?'

'That's what's so terrible for you. I'm sorry, sorry, so sorry.'

'But what for?' She was muscling over the desk now. Looked like a black sumo-wrestler. 'We're waiting for it. Your point.'

'Well, I mean. Like,' I said.

'You keep saying like, but like what?'

'What?' I said.

'What is like what? You keep saying, "I mean" but you don't say what you mean. You keep saying "like" but you don't say like what. What do you mean? What is it like?'

I let my tongue loll out at her, making myself look 'mentally challenged'. To wit, mongoloid.

She couldn't believe it. Could I be doing it on purpose? Could this possibly mean what it seemed to mean? Caught in a fury of uncertainty, she found herself pounding the table. With *both* fists.

'Are you? Are you! Can you be, can you really be poking your tongue out? At me!'

I dragged my tongue back in. A sheer effort of will, though traumatized, isn't that the word, Squeezers? I showed her the trauma in my eyes. My lips did a bit of quivering.

'I'm sorry, sorry, so sorry about my tongue. Ever since I was a childhood, got frightened once, my father, he, he – and made me, made me lick, lick him with my tongue. And, and. He would order me to do it. And I was frightened. When he came into my bedroom, pulling his trousers down and pushing it at me, *it*. And me. I. Me. Knowing I had to lick it! So now, whenever somebody frightens me my tongue sticks out. Can't help it, Horatia, Horatia.'

Her rolls and chuckles and twinklings suddenly looked furtive. They, all of them, sickos and mark-grabbers, sort of passed. They passed on all this. What else could they do? The Corrector was all alone, on the burning bridge of sexual politics, about to crash, foaming, into the foam. Well, she shouldn't hang out with Esmé, should she, Twiskers? Her own fault. See?

'I didn't know, I'm, I'm, what can I – ?' She went back behind the desk. 'What can I do? To make amends. You poor, poor, what a, a –' she groped around – 'monster.'

Pathetic, really. Couldn't she see how easy? But panic destroys, or something.

'He was a good man except for that. And he loved me. He did. Yes, he did. It wasn't his fault. He was – was – the same thing happened to him, you see. By his uncle. Old Ted. He used to stay at the weekends. Dad. My Dad told me. It wasn't his fault he frightened me and made me stick my tongue out and lick him.' I stuck my tongue out at her.

She had nowhere to go, really. She was crumpled, all

fat and dark, in her chair. She looked at Sally, at Ms Piggy, at the others in the room, and she made a crooning noise.

'That's the classical story. Child-abuse begets child-abuse, from generation into generation.'

The Caribbean rhythm got into her voice again, but this time all the way back to her childhood, church-teaching and stuff.

'He died of cancer when I was twelve,' I said.

'Yes, well.' She peered about. Not even the sickos would meet her eyes. 'Yes, well. Class dismissed,' she came up with.

In all the time I've been at the Dump I've never heard those words: 'Class dismissed'. In all the time Horatia the Corrector has been at the Dump she's never uttered them. 'Class dismissed.' Think of it. And five minutes early at that.

Dismissed, we left. Horatia did some headless-chicken rolling, heaving, chortling, but nobody glanced at her. Except me. I stuck my tongue out at her one last time.

The thing about Helena Twiscombe's room, *Dr* Twiscombe's room, is the reek of furtive smoking. And there's also the reek of alcohol. Gin, I think. But my nostrils are too innocent to distinguish between gin, vodka and whisky, say. But she probably keeps a bottle of one of those in a drawer.

I sat down and waited. I closed my eyes and there she was, Sissy, first beneath my eyelids and then filling the whole of me. I didn't hear the door open. I must have moaned the name aloud.

'What?' she barked as she waddled in. She was carrying the usual sheaf of papers, with her usual look of bewildered irritation – as if there were an unlocatable mosquito in the room. She stamped clumsily around her desk, slapped the papers on it, then gave a long, blinking stare. Straight at me.

'Are you all right? You look very flushed and in some disarray.'

I refrained from glancing down to b.t.l. I go on the principle that nothing ever shows. Live by it.

'Sorry, Dr Twiscombe. I've been far away,' I said humbly. 'I was thinking about my dead twin, you see.'

She sat down heavily, almost with a kind of bump. 'I thought when we were doing Wordsworth, and I was talking about loss, the poetry of loss, and I asked you if you'd had any personal experience of loss, you said no, you were an only child. Everybody you'd ever known is still alive. I remember quite distinctly as I thought you were a trifle pert. Pert and dismissive. Just like an only child.'

You're not only clever, Twiscombe, you've got a memory.

'I am now,' I said, humbly still.

'Am now what, are you?'

'Am now an only child. Since my twin's death.'

'But you've never known loss.'

Her stare was coming straight at me again. This time without blinks. There was a grin in her eyes. She'd been trying for weeks to catch me out.

'I didn't lose him. He was going as I was coming, you see.'

'Then why were you thinking about him?'

'He just popped into my head. What it would have been like to have another self. To be connected umbili-cally.'

35

'You wouldn't have been connected umbilically. That's with the mother. Surely you know *that* much. Under the circumstances.'

I was ahead of her. Leaking out some pain.

'No, well, you see, you see – my parents, well, they never talk about him. I think it's still a sore point.'

'A sore point!' She let out a *bellow* of laughter. Never heard that before. 'Losing a child! A *sore* point!'

'With me,' I said, looking at her, puzzled. 'A sore point that they never discussed him with me. Ever.'

She was in like a whippet. 'And yet you know.'

'Except that once,' I sped on, ahead of her again. 'Just that once.'

Now here was an invitation, Twiskers. Lots of tears coming up if you wanted them. I certainly wanted them – needed them – if I was going to get what I really needed and wanted. I could see the temptation there all right. Just one question would do it. 'What happened that once?' That's all she had to ask.

She hesitated, then shook her head either at me or at herself.

'It's time to do some work.' She plucked an essay out of a file. Mine all right.

'This is,' she said, 'this is.' She held it up and blinked, gazed and, yes, actually glared at it.

'Rubbish?' I offered.

'Yes. No. Yes and no. My belief is that you're a phoney. And a liar.'

She watched me as tears hovered, excruciatingly, at the rims of my eyes, or wherever tears hover. Then they receded. Apart from three. Two from my left eye, if you're facing me. One from the right. Or the other way around, if you're me.

'Phoney?' Twiscombe (Dr) enquired, genuinely inquisitive.

'I don't cry to requirement.'

'I wasn't requiring you to cry.'

'No. You *made* me cry. But I stopped myself.'

'Why? Why not let it out. If it's really true.'

'Dr Twiscombe –'

'I'm Helena.'

'Helena?'

'I'd prefer it if you called me Helena.' The stare and the blinks suddenly went all over the place. 'It's my first name,' she said meaninglessly. Then she wagged my essay, also meaninglessly. See how quickly I pick up on your emotions, Twiskers? Even when you express them meaninglessly.

'Helena. Thank you, Helena. It's very kind. The reason I choked back, *checked* my tears, Helena, is.' I stopped. Quite deliberately stopped. And waited.

'Well then! Explain!'

'I'm not going to be harassed into crying for you. I'm not, Helena.'

With everyone else in the Dump, Left-Overs, Deansy-Weansy, the Corrector, etc., you only have to say, merely imply 'harassed', and up goes the white flag, in is thrown the towel. With Twiskers, it's a call to arms. 'Harassed?'

'Well, isn't being called a phoney and a liar a kind of harassing – ?'

She smiled. I like her smile. She's got good teeth, but that's not it. She's got good, clean teeth in a handsomely, strongly, honestly flabby and puffy face. That's not it. No, what it is is (that looks terrible, 'is is', as terrible as 'was was' was) that in spite of that expression I described earlier, the irritated bewilderment stuff, she's got the nicest face. But you only see that when you smile, Sissy. I mean Twiskers. Everything else about you vanishes and you see – oh yes, what you see is the smile of a child. That's it. Of a child who hasn't learnt yet that there are occasions when she *has* to smile. No corruption in it.

'Are you thinking,' she said, 'of going to the Dean and accusing me of harassment?' And there was the smile as she said it. Not the hint of a fear or a jeer. A child asking. With pleasure. I didn't know what to say. The smile *did* undo me.

'Well,' she barked intimately, no boom in it. 'If you do I won't mind. I'll admit it. I'm trying to harass you. Harass you into honesty.'

'All right,' I said.

'All right. What does that mean? In this context?'

'Well, go ahead. Harass me into honesty. If you can.'

'I need your help. Or rather, let's say complicity. In your case. If we begin by thinking it's a conspiracy between us, full of deceit. And work our way towards honesty.'

'How?'

'By finding a way for you to *enjoy* telling the truth. Later, of course, when you can do it, it'll become more painful.'

'But if it becomes painful?'

'Why tell the truth? You find out more. And that's interesting. You find out more about yourself. And other people.'

'I *did* have a dead twin!'

'That's right.' She nodded in approval. 'You did have. A few minutes ago.'

'And you want to take him away from me? Is that it? Even if I only imagine a twin it's just because I *want*, I *need*, I *need*, I *want* –' I stared at her helplessly, 'in loss'.

Bingo! A poisoned arrow right to the heart.

Her eyes seemed to dissolve into a mess. And everything else about her seemed to dissolve into a mess. A mess behind a desk, that's what Twiskers suddenly became, didn't you, Whiskers, eyes and all?

'Want, need, need, want,' she whispered it out to herself. 'You're quite right. Everyone is entitled to their, their imaginings, I suppose. After all, without them no poetry, no art of any kind, and then what would we have? Nothing. I'm sorry. Insensitive and stupid of me.' It came out in a mumble of shame, eyes blinking down at the desk.

'That's all right,' I said, 'that's all right. You mustn't – you mustn't –'

She looked at me quickly, too quickly. I don't know whether she caught the triumph in my eyes but even if she did it was too late.

'Thank you,' I said. 'Thank you for understanding. How's Sissy?'

'Sissy?'

'Your niece, Sissy. That I met at the Dean's reception.' I was getting towards my lisp. Did I have the nerve? 'She'th from Authtralia, ithn't she? What doeth she do while she'th here, vithiting you?'

'What young women do when they look in on their aunts in London.'

'Oh, tho you don't know then, you mean. How she thpendth her dayth.'

She let the lisp pass. I mean, what could she do

except keep up the social pitter-patter her shame had lured her into. She went into a ramble about what Sissy had done yesterday, tennis in the morning, lunch with friends, the National Gallery in the afternoon, what she was doing today, lunch with friends, on to the Sickert exhibition at the Tate, and then she (the Waddler itself) was taking her to *Carmen* –

'The Sickert?' I said.

'Yes, there's an exhibition at the Tate, I don't know why she wants to see Sickert, some of the early stuff is fine, I suppose, but the later, I can't believe that Sissy will enjoy –' she stopped. 'But why on earth are we talking about – about my niece?' Her hands were trembling, her jowls (or were they wattles?) enlarging. 'Why do I always let you make these tutorials so *personal*?'

'Personal?' I almost said 'perthonal'. 'Really? I'm so sorry.' Nearly 'thorry'. Nearly 'tho', come to that. 'I don't mean to.'

Her laugh, intended to be a barking boom of derision, came out as a croak.

'You *always* mean to be personal. You don't know how to be anything else. In fact, that's *all* you know. And you do it by lies, tricks – this essay, this essay about Byron is personal. *Perthonal*,' she mimicked. 'You talk about him as if you were his – his –' Her face and voice throbbed in disgust. I knew what the disgust came from. 'Slimey,' she said. 'A clever, deceitful, slimey piece of writing. Thlimey.' She was almost crying. She muttered something.

'Sorry, Helena, I didn't quite –'

She looked up and there was, well, actually, there was either fear or hate there. Or both.

'Oh, go away. Please go away. Go!'

I got up, briefly wondered what would happen if I did what I wanted to do, realized I'd only know if I did it. I slipped behind her, bent over her as she bent over the desk. I let my hand drift around the back of her head. Inches away, I could feel the ample folds of her neck pulsing. My lips were close to her ear.

'Thank you for taking so much trouble just for me, Helena,' I whispered. I bent closer.

She sat there in dread, waiting for me to speak again.

I opened my lips, closed them, making a popping sound that could have been a kiss.

I don't think she heard me move on around her and cross her room to the door. Or the door opening and closing.

I walked a few steps down the hall, then slid back, peered through the frosted glass windows. Although her movements were blurred, I understood them perfectly. The opening of the drawer, the bottle straight to her lips and kept there for a long, long time, then the other drawer and a cigarette. She slumped forward, bottle in one hand, cigarette in the other, and tears – I couldn't see them of course, but it's true, isn't it, Waddler? Tears splattering down on to your blouse? She looked up suddenly as if knowing that my eyes were on her, meeting hers through the fuzzy glass. She bowed her head.

I turned away down the corridor, light-footed, young, free. Out of the Dump. On to the Tate.

The Waddler had got Sickert right on the button. But you would, wouldn't you, PhDone-for, being a great critic of everything but yourself. I mean, how could a guy who did *those* paintings – there's one of a man singing in a music hall, arm over his chest, singing and staring up into the gallery, and you see the woman in the gallery, among all the people in the gallery you see the one, the only woman he's looking at, and you can make up a whole story from it, that's what's nice, that the story of the picture somehow moves on, you try to hear his song, feel her pride in being singled out, wonder what they've already done together, what they'll get up to when they're by themselves again – I mean, how could a guy who did *that* end up churning out enormous portraits of the famous dead?

And suddenly she's there, Sissy. She gives me a quick glance, not recognizing me because I'd been very cunning with her at the reception. A creepy little thing I'd been, hunched, almost wizened, keeping my eyes averted so that she wouldn't see the sparkling knowledge in them. I'd leaked out a kind of mean-spirited insignificance while remaining mute. But now, now, I can feel all over my skin her inner eye feasting itself on me, even though her outer eye is busy on the art-appreciation. She's wearing a grey silk dress, to just below the knee. And a black cloak, half-length, to protect her against the nip of spring, but hanging loosely from one shoulder as it's warm in here, grey high-heels that aren't too high because of her height.

She has her hands on her hips, almost as if in indignation, her head thrust forward, but about to turn away. I can sense it, the impatience but the dutifulness, she's going to look properly at this ghastly tinted photograph of a famous dead, but get it over with as soon as possible. She turns her head to see what corpse is coming up next, her hair, corn-coloured, almost to her

42

shoulders, swings. I move in, stand beside her, not seeing her, but feeling her feel me at her side.

I moan.

That light voice is as silky as her dress.

'I'm sorry – but are you all right?'

I give a kind of jump. Start, I suppose it is. A start.
Look at her startled, after my start, amazed that there is
someone beside me. Accosting me.

'I'm sorry?'

'It's just that you sounded as if you might be ill.'

'Oh.' I'm shy and polite, but cautious. As if more
could be going on here. Like a pick-up even. 'Well, a little bit ill.'

'Oh. Oh, dear.' She made it sound slightly old-fashioned. 'What – ? Is there anything I can –?' Usual stuff.

'Honestly –' I said, 'honestly, it's too ridiculous. Yes.
Silly. I'm being silly. It's –' I nodded at the picture,
winced. 'It's that, you see. It's probably I mean great. I
dunnow anythink –' That's going too far. Might put her
off. I wind back a bit, step up a class or two. 'I don't
know too much about pictures. Art. I'm trying to learn
and, and all I know is I liked all that stuff in there and
came in here and there was this. These. And I wondered what happened to him. Something terrible.'

'Success,' she said. Her eyes were on me now. Grey
eyes, with feeble vision. Not seeing clearly. But not
squinty. No, not in the slightest squinty.

'Oh,' I said, 'so he couldn't really help it.' I gave her
the old ingenuous, with a flicker of frightened wit.

She chortled. Some women really chortle, they really
do, not like Horatia, the Corrector, but a real burst of
pleasure from the throat it sounds like, more than a
laugh. I love genuinely chortling women. Beautiful

women with long legs and proud breasts and straight backs, chortling straight into your face almost. Her breath was sweet, of course, but there it was, the faint whiff or stain of it. Exciting.

'I think I've got to go outside,' she said.

'To have a cigarette?'

She blinked. Or no. Her eyelids did a little flutter, not for me. Quite involuntary.

'How did you know?'

'Your breath.'

'Oh, no!' she said. And blushed. The dab of pink rising on each cheek.

'But it's only because I smoke too, you see,' I said, 'that I recognize the smell.'

That's fatuous. Fatuous. It's non-smokers who recognize the smell, smokers don't notice it, as it's around them all the time. It's the air they breathe. It's their shroud.

'I'm a smoker who's given up smoking, you see. Like an alcoholic who's given up drink. So I'm sensitive to the smell.'

Her smile, which had been a lingering business, tightened. Voice iced up a bit. No chortle. 'I'm sorry,' she said. 'How awful for you.'

'No, I love it, love it! The very faintest, delicatest whiff – I still *want* to smoke, so I like to, well, stand close to people who are smoking. Just to catch a trace.' There. 'And on you it's tantalizing. Such a tantalizing hint.' We turned and walked through the gallery together. We were going past those clusters of people, in one of which two of whom (one of them a man) wore woolly hats.

Outside, on the top step of the Tate, she plunged her

hand into her cape pocket and pulled out a packet of Silk Cut. She inspected it casually. She was now in a position to smoke, so there was no urgency. She put a cigarette between her lips, let it hang there, took out a book of matches, bent one of the matches back, flicked it across the black strip, hand cupped, lit up.

I hovered over her, sniffing and inhaling. Hovered over her, but still kept a proper and polite distance between us.

She smiled, held the cigarette out, towards my nostrils. 'Why don't you have one?'

'Because then I'll have another and another, and –'

'And it'll damage your health.'

'Oh, I don't care about that! It's just that I can't afford them. You see – you see –'

And I stumbled into an incoherently lucid account of what it's like to be fresh out of drama school with no work in sight, though I'd got an agent who was interested in me, I might be going up for some parts soon, etc., etc., but what it comes to is that I'm on the dole, every penny or p. counting. I did, truly, keep all element of self-pity out of my voice. Quite hard, when you're lying, because you have to *see* the plight you're making up for yourself, and it's a pitiful one.

She listened with graceful attention, *her* lungs welcoming whatever it is is welcoming in nicotine and smoke.

But actually, actually, she was more with me than with her cigarette. And that was good. Her captivity was coming along nicely, nicely. The first stage, anyway.

'So where do you live?'

'Oh, not far – I suppose you wouldn't want – would you?'

45

'What?'

I made a lovely stammering and stuttering noise. She looked at me with affection. I was a darling little stray of a dog she'd chanced across.

'What wouldn't I want?'

'I can make tea. Coffee too. I've got some drink. Port, I think it is. Or sherry. One of those. I won it in a lottery at drama school. We all had to enter and I won this bottle of brownish.' I stood, fawn-like, before her, letting her see my expectation of rebuff, which glowed at her, enticingly.

'You don't drink either, then?'

'Well, only with someone,' I ducked my head, 'I've been waiting for.'

'Waiting for?' A cool lift of the eyebrow. 'I wouldn't mind a cup of coffee. But I'll have to be quick. My aunt's taking me to *Carmen*. Do I really have time?'

She looked at her watch. Proper numbers on a large, manly face, broad strap, I'm glad to report. 'How far is it?'

'Oh, twenty minutes, half an hour on foot at the most.'

She signalled a taxi, which was depositing Muslims meanwhile.

'We'll go in one of these, if you don't mind. It's on me.'

'No, no,' I trotted at her side. 'I really can't allow –'

'Yes, you can.' She opened the door. 'Where are we going? The address?'

I told the driver and climbed in.

So there I was, PhDog, sitting in the taxi. Your Sissy beside me. Driving away from the Tate towards the destination I'd had in mind for her from the first moment I saw her. Her long, black-stockinged legs are showing beneath her grey dress – her slightly hiked grey dress – one of these legs is very nearly pressing against mine, which is just as long (and shapely) as hers.

'Have you got a telephone?' she asked.

'No. No. I'm sorry.'

'How will I get a cab?' That's her class. She says cab and not taxi. 'I'll need to get a cab back.'

'Oh, you can phone for one.'

'Where from? I hope it's not one of those that takes phone cards only. Mine's just run out. Have I got any change?' She fumbles in her cloak pocket, opens her purse, peers into it anxiously. Women look so charming when they have to peer short-sightedly for practical purposes.

'Why do you need change?' I was anxious myself, of course. Anxious and bewildered.

She almost snapped it at me. 'For the telephone, what else?'

I became seriously damaged. Shrivelled with hurt, shrunk with shame. 'But I wouldn't charge you for using my telephone, I wouldn't do that!'

'You said you didn't *have* a telephone!'

'No, in my flat I do – I thought you meant here. Now. In my pocket. One of those that those people, you know, carry about – I thought – I thought that you know those sort of people and just assumed that I was one of those.'

'Oh.' A flash of suspicion, then the chortle again. More like a guffaw, which is, in my judgement, a chortle out of control.

'No, I'm not one of those.' She moved her leg an inch closer, or further away, one or the other.

47

'I'm glad.'

'Why?'

'Well, I'd feel *completely* out of my depth.'

She peered into my eyes. Yes, she did. Her short-sighted grey eyes *peered* into my long-visioned blue ones. Blue flecked with grey, they tell me. There were no flecks of blue in hers. They were luminously grey.

'Are you – ?' She did something quizzical with her eyebrows. They were – oh, to hell with her eyebrows. I was too busy being aware of the calf, its closeness, under the grey dress.

'Am I what?' I turned, looked studiously out of the window.

She said nothing. I could hear my own breathing. My knee was breathing at her knee. I was going wet, disturbingly wet, b.t.l.

'Taking me for a ride?'

'Oh!' I turned to her, aghast. 'I can't afford – I just haven't enough. I thought *you* were going to – to –'

'Stop it.' She slapped the knee next to hers, which was mine of course. 'Not another word until we get there.' She turned to look through her window. I turned to look through mine. Our legs were close again. So close. But not touching. No. She swung hers away. She lit a cigarette. I heard it. Smelt it.

The window between ourselves and the driver slid open.

'Hey, look, there it is!' His free hand reached back and rapped at the 'Thank you for not smoking' sign.

'That's all right,' she growled calmly. And went on smoking, calmly.

He tried to slam the window back with a bang, but couldn't. It slid along, grooved, and there was just his

48

head, poked forward in fury, his neck mottled with it.

She growled some more, looking out of her window. Our knees longed to be in touch. Otherwise silence.

When we got there she does this thing. What she does is this. She gives the taxi driver what's on the meter, nothing more. He looks at her, starts to say something, meets her blankly lovely, obstinate eyes. There is the shortest of tussles.

'Thank *you*, madam,' he says, and sulks his taxi off.

'So this is where you live?'

It's quite grand. Large house on the Embankment, a large house among a terrace of large houses, nannies on the pavement with the children, one or two civil servants sauntering past in the late spring sunshine, back early from their offices or from their adulteries or whatever. The little iron gate, the path to the front door, a tree overhanging it.

'You live here then?'

I bustled forward, took out the keys, opened the dark, narrow door with the Chubb. Triple-locked it is, so I had to do it thrice, twice above and once below.

'This way.' I continued my bustle, past the steep, curving staircase, to the door at the end of the passage. 'This one's mine.' I put in the Yale, opened the door, stood beside it as she glided past me, cloaked and in grey, the scent of her, her heels rapping on the tiles.

'Oh,' she said. She looked around as I shut the door. Yaled her in with my key.

'It's lovely. Lovely. I'd no idea. From what you said. No idea that it would be so lovely.' She was staring around, alarmed by her own surprise. There were the little drawings in the hall, delicate of line and brush. There were the little water-colours in the hall, punctuated by the occasional charcoal drawing. All of them in some ways images of freedom. The usual bird in flight. A salmon leaping up the falls. A boy running down a long, sloping hill, effortlessly running, head thrown back, mouth open, arms partly stretched. You could *hear* the glee from his throat with your eyes. And the ship in full sail, flying, flying. I raced ahead, desperate to get her into *my* room. No. *Our* room. I flung it open, the door, and stood, head drooping, to let her by me. The sound of silk flowing, the high-heels rapping gently. And she's in.

She looked from long wall to long wall, then through the French windows to the garden. She took out a cigarette, lit it.

'No wonder you gave up smoking,' she said. 'If it helps you to afford a place like this.'

'Oh, it's not mine,' I said, gesturing awkwardly to a chair.

'I'd like a chance to look for a moment. If I may.'

'Yes. Yes, you may.'

Our eyes met. She shifted away, towards all those paintings.

I pointed to the telephone, a clumsy black original from circa 1950, not a fraudulent graced-up copy. 'What else would you like?'

'Only an ash-tray. This carpet. I wouldn't want to get ash on it.'

'Oh, don't worry. She won't mind. As a matter of fact she smokes herself. She says ash is "positively good" for carpets. Ash and champagne give carpets more texture, she says.'

I was doing spasms of imitation on the champagne and ash stuff. Difficult, as I didn't know who I was imitating. I'd got no kind of fix on what to tell her about my 'landlady'. Who she was, or what our relationship was. I think there was a dash of West Country in the 'champagne' though.

She was studying Burochini (well, some name like that. Or school of some name like that). The triptych of Perseus and Andromeda. What *is* a triptych? Three panels put together with hinges, to tell a story. Anyway, that's what it was. My Sissy was studying the triptych of Perseus and Andromeda. In the middle panel Andromeda is chained to the rock. On the left Perseus is riding his winged horse towards her, to rescue her. On the right Perseus is riding his winged horse away from her, probably having just done a routine check on the chains.

'Where is she?' she said.

'Oh, well, on a rock, isn't she? Somewhere in Greece.'

'Ah. And when's she coming back?'

'Oh, I suppose when he decides to let her go.'

She turned her head, hair swinging, towards me. Then, realizing, looked back at the pictures. 'No, no –' A guffaw this time. 'I meant whoever the *she* is who owns all this. You mentioned a "she".' She'd moved on to the St George and the Dragon, painted under the personal supervision of Gblzo (Polish, 17th century) by one of his students, a Turkish lad, I believe. There she is, chained to the tree, while St George and the Dragon are consulting closely together, gossiping almost, about the stock market. Or her price. No, not her price, there's no air of haggling about either of them. Old chums, enjoying each other's company. The lady's head is on the droop, the arms stretched upwards –

'I still need an ash-tray.'

51

I handed her something like an ash-tray, but antique and precious. Chinese?

'I can't really use that!' She was genuinely shocked.

'Why not?'

'Well, it's wood, isn't it?'

'Is it?' I inspected it. Tapped it. 'Yes, you're right. Wood. Well, what about this?' I cupped my hand and held it out towards her.

Our eyes locked? Our eyes met? Anyway, we stood staring into each other's eyes.

'Who is your "she"?' This was huskily done. She tapped ash into my cupped palm.

'You are,' I said shyly. 'Aren't you? You're my "she".'

It was quite a challenge, really, this business of which one would drop our eyes.

'I'm not the she of yours that lets you live in this flat. Where shall I stub this out?'

'Wherever you like.' I kept my hand cupped.

'You like pain, do you?'

'Hate it.' This is true.

She took a last drag on the cigarette, inhaled, and moved the butt down towards my cupped hand.

I closed my eyes. I felt the heat of the tip almost in my palm. Then the muffled click of her heels on the carpet, sensed the flow of movement away from me, then the sharp click of her heels on the flagstones outside the French windows. I raised my lids a trifle. There was the simple garden furniture, white and iron, under the green shade of the tree, surrounded by the green of the grass, the bursting spring flowers. And there was this grey loveliness, this grey thought in a green shade, tapping her butt out – no, no! – stubbing the butt, grinding out her butt, anyway putting out the remnants of her cigarette in the large, triangular, yellow ash-tray that advertises that clear stuff that goes all cloudy when you put ice or water in it. Pernod.

She was coming back through the French windows. Click-click, then no sound. My eyes were still closed. My hand still out, cupped. I could feel my own moisture and her dignified dampness.

'There,' she said. 'All done. You can open your eyes now. If you want.'

'I'm not sure,' I said. 'Afraid.'

'Of what?'

'Of you. What will I see, when I open my eyes?'

'Me. Just me. Nothing else.'

I opened my eyes.

'Well then, who is this "she" of yours?'

'A friend. An old friend.'

'Ah. Old *friend*? Or an *old* friend?'

'Of the family.'

'But which? Is she *old* or is she a friend of long –'

'A kind of patroness,' I muttered. 'I mean, when she's away for a long period she lets me use this place.' Well, I couldn't possibly tell her the truth about the house, how I got the keys, could I? Too complicated and unsavoury really. She struggled with herself for a moment, then decided to drop the subject.

'And please put your hand back where it belongs.'

'Where does it belong?'

'Anywhere but in a begging position. Do you want coins? Is that it?'

'Not coins.'

'What then? What *do* you want?' I could smell her, feel her, inches away from me. The long-legged shape of her waist down the slender torso, the trusting – no, the *thrusting!* breasts. And there is this thing, you see, about the mouths of really beautiful women. They go on past where they should stop. The lips have a lift and a mild, amused curve to them. Humour, radiance, an inner life all there in the extra of the lips. The curve, naturally, going just a fraction upwards. Or no. Going *naturally* upwards.

'I want you,' I said. A fact. I wanted her. 'I want you.'

'Yes,' she said. 'And your *patroness*.' She couldn't help it. 'Does *she* want you?'

'I promised her,' I said, 'I'd never talk about her. I promised.' I smiled honourably.

She raised a hand. Then, with effort, sort of stroked her chin.

Small, rounded chin. But firm. Almost obstinate.

'How long can you stay?' I got some husky into my own voice.

'Until I phone for my cab.'

'What do *you* want?'

One of the loveliest pauses of my life.

'I want you.'

'Oh, gosh!' Yes. That's what I actually said. 'Oh, gosh.'

'Oh, gosh! Oh, gosh!' Imitating me, possibly accurately. 'Oh, gosh! What does that *mean*?'

'Well, you want me.' I stumbled through this. 'And I want you.'

'Then it's easy enough, isn't it? We both want the same thing. So why don't we –'

'I don't think we do necessarily, necessarily, want the same thing. I mean I may want this.' I gestured. 'You may want,' I gestured, 'that.'

She suddenly hated me, from the pit of her desire. Why? After all, she was going to get *something*. She wanted *something*, and I'd give her *something*, though probably not what she thought she wanted, it's true.

'How do we resolve our dilemma?'

'Play a little game. Winner takes all.'

'All of what?'

'All of me, if you win. All of you, if I win.'

'For how long would you have all of me, if you won?'

'Oh –' slack and easy, 'until you phone for a taxi to take you to your Auntie for *Carmen*.'

'And for how long will I have you?'

'For as long as you want.'

'So you have me until I call for a cab?'

I nodded.

'But I have you for as long as I want?'

I nodded.

She nodded. 'What's the game?' She took out her cigarettes.

I took them from her with immense gentleness. 'Nothing like this until it's over. Is that all right? In the rules?'

'I don't know any games. At least I don't *think* I do.' She looked like a child. 'There's snakes and ladders.'

'What about scissors cuts paper and paper covers stone and stone smashes scissors? Do you know *that* game? We do it simultaneously. With our fingers and hands,' I said. 'Two fingers out-stretched for Sissers and if you simultaneously put your hands out straight as I put out Twiskers you're paper and I cut you –'

'But if I put out my fists –'

'You smash Twiskers.'

'But if I hold out my palms, that's paper. If you hold out your fists I cover you.'

55

'You cover me.'

It was easy to control her defeats, her victories. All I had to do was to cheat. Instead of my show of fist, palm, fingers coinciding with her show of whatever, I in fact followed her by a fraction of a fraction of a second. Just time to make adjustments. But I let her win twice, for her pride's sake. Gave her those two, while awarding myself three.

'I win then,' I said at the end of the game. 'Take off your dress.'

She unbuttoned the three buttons at the top, then trying not to make a production of it, pulled her dress over her head.

So there she almost was. Over her round and pointy breasts a light web of black lace. Then the light pink skin of her torso. A black slip.

'The slip.'

She stepped out of her slip. As with the dress, she didn't fold or smooth, merely dropped it. She lowered her arms into a curious position. Not a demure maiden covering breasts and/or crotch, but a mature young woman trying, with dignity, not to behave like a demure maiden.

'This isn't fair,' she said. 'Not fair.'

'If you want permission to speak, stick out your tongue.'

'Stick out my —' She wrestled with herself. Honour won.

'Off with the bra.'

It's one of those bras that unclips at the front, between the breasts. She looked at me fleetingly, resentfully, longing to speak, but determined not to stick her tongue out. Her hands went to her bra, her fingers unclipped it, and down it fell. Her arms went back to her side without instruction. Her nipples! Oh God, her *nipples*! They were plump and dainty, brown and – and – 'Odd,' I said. 'Briefs is plural. But the thing itself is singular. So take off the singular garment that we refer to in the plural.'

The fingers plucked them or it wide, and she stepped gracefully out of it or them. Or would have, if the heel of her left-hand high-heel hadn't caught on the cloth. She stumbled slightly; readjusted her position, one knee bent up, one leg lurching but anchored. Off it or they came. Down on the floor they and it went.

What a scattering of clothes! The dress spread, the bra on top of it, the slip on the other side of her, the miserly but rewarding briefs in front of her. And she, standing, fists clenched to her sides, the breasts thrusting, the long torso, and her navel! I haven't taken in your niece's navel and offered it to you, have I, Twiskers, old bean? It's a neat, uncomplicated whorl, with the slightest suggestion of grit in it. A little plughole of a navel, the grit effect coming from – oh, I don't know, specks of cloth from the slip. No. The slip is *below* the navel, so the grit is from nature, delicate specks of wart. She didn't know what to do with her head. Hang it, like the lady in St George and the Dragon. Hold it proudly high, at an almost unbearable angle, with an unbearable strain, like Andromeda on her rock. So she wagged it a bit, wagging her hair, just a bit of wagging, indecisive. The tongue was out.

'Not yet,' I said. 'Perhaps soon.'

The tongue went back in. She was furious. A furiously good loser.

There's something about a woman, especially a

mature and conceited, even patronizing woman, in gum-sticking stockings and high-heels and nothing else at all.

I eyed that little bush, thick and lovely bush of surprisingly dark hair at her crotch. She watched me, then looked down involuntarily, as men sometimes look down to check their flies.

'No, no,' I said. 'Up. Look up. As you were!' An old army phrase, I believe. 'As you were!'

She almost refused. Then did it. Out stuck the thumb. *Tongue*! I mean.

'Go ahead,' I nodded, myself the patronizing one. 'Fire away.'

'I want to go to bed with you. All right? But not in stockings and high-heels. Au naturel.' She turned the gaze away from me, swung her head slightly.

'Au naturel? That's not the same as vin ordinaire, is it?'

'What's the time?' she asked.

'Have a look,' I said. 'You're allowed. I allow you.'

She looked at her manly watch. 'Thirteen minutes. That's all you've got left of me.'

'Take it off,' I said.

She took it off her wrist, threw it on to the pile of clothing she'd stripped herself of, so that it landed safely.

'I'll tell you what. This matter of what you're wearing. I like you as you are. I could certainly live with that. But *you* choose. More? Or less? Which do you prefer?'

'Under the circumstances,' she said as if she'd sprung a trap, 'more.'

'OK. Okey-dokey.'

She bent to pick up her clothes, reaching, I noticed, for her watch first.

'Oh, no. Straighten up.' Her hand hovered over her watch. She straightened up. 'I've got something else for you. Don't worry. Very chaste.'

'Twelve minutes by now, I should think.'

'No more speech.' I took a slight extra breath here. 'Move your legs apart.'

A breath from her. She inched her right leg sideways.

'A little more,' I said judiciously, a master-craftsman of the old school.

She inched and inched. And inched.

'That's it,' I said when her legs were at the right distance from each other.

She was standing with her back to the cupboard, just far enough away for me to open the door. I'd arranged her exactly there so I wouldn't have to trek backwards and forwards with this item and that.

'And of course you're not to turn your head.' I opened the cupboard door, again a fine piece of Chinese something or other this cupboard is. *Chinoiserie.* 18th century? With a squeaking door.

'Oh.' I surveyed the contents. 'And close your eyes.' I didn't check. She'd have closed them all right. Besides, to have checked I'd have had to have walked around her and my attention was entirely divided between her buttocks.

I took down the belt. Not the gold one, the silver one. So no padlocks. With the silver all the ends slotted into each other, *locked* into each other, with a very delicate keyhole at the point where they locked.

I only had to turn and I was behind her. Around her waist it went. Click. I heard the murmur, Twiskers,

59

even as I slipped the silver band, padded with velvet for comfort where it counted, between your niece's legs and click.

'There. I told you it was chaste.' My tone was light, my hands were shaking. 'Chaste *and* snug. You couldn't be safer, could you?' I stepped around in front of her. She must have sensed me coming. Her eyes were closed. Her tongue was out.

'Not yet,' I said. 'Perhaps we'll have time for a snatch of chat before you go. Eh?' I wondered if she had any sensation of the cuffs that hung from the belt, swinging level with her pubic hair. They were slim, these cuffs, slim bracelets, but she must have felt their presence surely, their light, graceful presence swinging silently.

I clapped the collar around her neck. It wasn't too tight, a perfect fit for a long elegant neck. An elegantly involuntary adornment for a long, elegant neck. Back I went to the front of her. The black ribbon trailed indolently between the two firmly curving hills.

Oh, Twiskers, I'm creating something breathtaking. But honestly, 'dark stream between two curving' – honestly!

But at the end of the ribbon, which hung between her *boobs* (that's more like it – boobs not hills, and ribbon not stream), is a witty device, a dainty and charmingly shaped, *heart*-shaped, you see, key-ring. The ribbon, attached to a little clasp in the collar, in the form of a plump and nude and beaming Cupid, complete with quiver and arrows around his shoulder, bow and arrow in his hands, made of pearls and those green ones. Garnets? Or are garnets the red ones? Anyway, a green and dark-red image of Cupid is the clasp, the ribbon descending from it to between her hillocks – tits!

Tits! Not hillocks! Tits! Boobs! And pearls that are his jolly eyes. And pearls around the whole, and the whole exquisite clasp of Cupid, no larger than a thumbnail, and from this flows the ribbon from the collar to the heart-shaped key-ring between the boobs, tits, Bristols, hillocks, titty-pops, Sissy-pops, who cares? As long as they're not Twisky-pops!

So that was the belt and the collar. *Is* the belt, the collar.

'Legs closer together.' I went back to the cupboard. 'And eyes still closed.' I plucked out the ankle-hobble. Silver again. Five links separating the one from the other.

'And closer.' I was in front of her again.

She moved her legs closer, as if bored.

'That's about it,' I said. 'Yes. That's it.' Her ankles were about three inches apart. There, in their high-heels, the stick-on stockings stuck high on her thighs, the silver chastity belt, the glimpse from below of the ribbon trailing between her breasts to the Cupid key-holder. I snapped the, let's call them anklets, shall we? above the tops of her moderate high-heels. Which were shiny grey. Have I mentioned her shoes, Twiskers, their colour? Grey? Yes, I have. When we were back in the Tate and the shoes were matching the dress she is no longer wearing. And so are now very touching, her shoes, as they no longer match, though 'indeed, yes, indeed!' make a striking contrast with the long black legs, the silver belt gleaming around her waist, the line of silver looping tautly between her loins, bisecting her pubic hair, her *pudenda*, oh, so thick and jungly and yet somehow with a cultivated, hortocultivated (is there such a word, Twis, or have I just invented it?) look to it.

61

Lovely, lovely, tawny, bushy and lovely and tawny. So her shiny, grey shoes are abitrary, they seemed – just a minute, I'll look it up. Here we are. *Arbitrary*. Right meaning, wrong spelling. There she stood in her arbitrary shoes, thigh-gumming stockings and silver chains. A delight to the eye. This gloatingly darting, lasciviously loving eye of mine. But from her point of view, though she didn't have one, *her* eyes being sealed shut, she probably thought I was merely decorating her, like a Christmas tree.

The chains around her ankles were wisps almost, but unbreakable, of silver. I clip the silver bracelets attached to her belt around her right wrist and left wrist. Or the other way around, depending on whether you're me or she. Me or her. No, I or she, I mean. Sorry, Pedant hD.

'Don't open your eyes,' I say. 'And no movement. Not an inch of any part of your body.'

I turn her, my arm around her, directing her to the mirror in the door. And then withdraw from the picture. Tell her to open her eyes. To gaze upon the image of herself, self-constricted. And *then*, of course, she sees the little key-holes, the links, and she jerks, ineffectually jerks, her wrists away from the belt. Her ankles – she can move them towards each other, not away.

My arms appear briefly over her shoulders, my arms only, my shoulders and my head not in the frame of the mirror. My fingers, with comical deftness, insert the key into the Cupid key-ring. It swings listlessly between her breasts. How I adore them, those breasts, the key hanging between them. Cupid, armed and useless, as her breasts actually heave. She has nothing else to heave except her breasts – hey, why not simply call them heavers, from now on? Yes. That settles *that* problem at last. Heavers.

So there. There she is. Not able to move an inch in any direction. Not sideways, forwards, backwards. Not tiring, exactly, at her age, even when on grey high-heels, in black stockings. Black stockings don't come into whether it's tiring or not. But the grey high-heels do. Stuck to the floor. Not exhausting, her enchaining into silver, her silvering into herself, perhaps, but very, very boring. Unless she likes the image. Likes the thought of my loving the image of only herself, chained to herself. And now her tongue sticking out at herself.

Twiskers, do you think I'm too literal, too repetitive? Think of Sickert's singer or these paintings here, for instance? They're what *you* call metaphors. They tell stories in a single image, or at the most, in a triptych of images, and yet here am I, puzzling and fretting over every minor facet of your niece's situation. Why can't *I* do the broad brush-strokes?

In a minute I'll go to the cupboard and take out the bit, the fine silver bit (*extremely* expensive, Aspreys or Tiffany's or one of those places), a bit that any horse would be proud to flash between its teeth, with soft leather padding at each end. Glitter and dental comfort both combined.

'No, no, no, please no!' she'll squawk. Basic squawk. She'll clamp her mouth shut.

I'll squeeze her nostrils. No. I'll caress her nostrils. Her mouth eventually, drooling deliciously, will open. In will go the bit. Her teeth will clamp down on the leather, the silver will glitter between her lips, the drool drool. After I've buckled it at the nape of her

63

neck I'll stand directly in front of her –

I stood directly in front of her. I saw myself obscured but visible in her unsquinting but myopically focused eyes. I saw her seeing me for what I was. I couldn't speak. Something was beginning. Something strange was beginning. A completely new feeling. So new that it was like little shocks, warm little shocks, to every part of me.

I unclipped the key from between her breasts – not heavers, not anything but my Sissy's breasts – and unlocked every lock as quickly as I could. Click, click, click, unlock, unlock, unlock.

She reached out, took my hand, led me to the bed. She undressed me slowly, as a nurse might. No, that's wrong. As an older sister might. Or an Auntie might. Tenderly. And I, like a child, obediently raising my arms for the leather jacket; the blouse after she'd done the unbuttoning; held my legs out for the unlacing of the trainers, the peeling-off of the socks; stood up as she drew down my jeans, raising each foot in my obedience; then of course for the 'them' or 'it', the singular and the plural. I knelt at her feet, took off her shoes and rolled down her stockings, while she stroked my hair.

That's how it goes on, Twiskers, every afternoon. We start with a game, more elaborate each time. Poker, vingt-et-un, draughts, chess, and backgammon. I don't cheat any more, so of course she always wins. And that's the right way round. I mean, what have I got to give her but me? My fine-boned wrists are cuffed together under my buttocks, those cheeky mounds that are no longer mine. One ankle is stretched to one post, the other to the other. I'm spread-eagled, available to whomever (correct? whomever?) but only *one*, *one* has the right of passage. She could invite friends to have a look, a lick, a nibble. But never does, my Sissy. I am too special. She couldn't bear, she tells me, to share me. Especially not with you, Whiskery Twiskery PhDumpling.

I shift my head the permitted inch, to look at the Dragon or Andromeda, who seem to be gossiping across to each other from painting to painting. Now and then she passes across the French windows, carrying an armload of assorted flowers.

'Please!' I whisper. 'Please!'

Mostly she just passes by, but now and then, now and then she murmurs –

'Not yet. In due course. But not yet. I'm busy, you see. Too busy to bother with you. But I'll find the time. Later.'

And later she comes through the French windows and sits down on the edge of the bed. She looks mildly distraught, as if she's done more than enough for one day, needs to put the day behind her. The three top buttons of her blouse are undone. I can see, when she bends towards me, her cleavage; the black satin of her bra.

'Are you good at singing?'

'No. I sing flat.'

She takes the key out of her pocket, revolves it almost irritably between her fingers.

'Sing anyway,' she says.

'No.' I turn my head away. The collar clinks softly. My hands curl into my buttocks, sharp-nailed.

She unlocks the strip between my legs, and puts her hand there, b.t.l. I am determined to make no sound, no sound.

She takes off her hat. She bends over me. All that long, silky blondiness is falling over my stomach, as she licks at me, and then with such craft, such guile, such *wit*, her tongue and lips playing all kinds of jokes with me. I writhe in my chains and I twist my collared neck about and about and I –

I hear it myself. Hear the note of it, the meaning of it. And the beginning of the surging, legs beginning to shake.

She padlocks me into myself again with a contemptuous little click.

'What do you feel?' She smiles down at me.

'You know what I feel.'

'You feel desperate.'

'If I said – if I said please – please. I can't be left like this.'

'Yes. You can. And are being. And the next time I ask you to sing to me, you'll sing to me. Won't you?'

I nod. Clink. Clink. 'I'll sing for you now.'

'Oh, you've sung enough. A few little notes. Not all of them flat.'

On the bed we romp, becoming merrier and merrier. In each other's arms we talk whisperingly to each other.

Your name comes up now and again, Waddler. Spooky's the word she uses. How spooky you've become. Spooky and lonely and give her the creeps. She never knows whether you're there or not, except from the smell.

I went with her once for a few moments so I could experience it for myself. The smell wasn't fresh, it wasn't stale, just the smell of *you*. We listened outside your door. We couldn't hear anything except what sounded like heavy breathing, the sort of noise you hear outside a room when there's somebody in it. Or nobody. We peeked through the window on the way out. You were at your desk, staring at us but seeming to see something else entirely. Then you got up. You waddled straight towards us, as if you were going to waddle your way through the window, through our clasp, and divide us. You retreated, waddling backwards. Retreated and sank bruisingly to your knees, into your darkness.

In the course of my reading, I'd come around the desk and stumbled to my knees, bruising them. Now I'm back behind my desk, my knees still throbbing but my mind clearing. I'm keeping my hand away from my glass, which is almost empty. And I'm keeping the glass away from the bottle which I've put in a drawer. I've made one decision. From now on I shall keep a record of everything I do. Hour by hour. Minute by minute, if possible. Anyway, there'll always be a pad about my person. If, and God forbid, God forbid, I should suffer any more memory losses I shall be able to consult my pads, and fill myself in. I shall know everything I've done by simply turning to these pads. As for the pile of filth on my desk, I've just written on it, 'The author of these pages is Helena Twiscombe' – (notice the omission of 'Dr' and 'PhD') – 'written when in a state of moral and emotional collapse.' And underneath that I've added, in block capitals, the single word 'DRUNK'. There. Over and done with. Needless to say I crossed out the 'grateful student' and 'In Memoriam'. This addition and subtraction of a few words has increased my calm. My knees, too, are beginning to quieten down. I'm in the right state to go to a meeting at last. I shall speak. I'll write it down. 'Helena, you've promised me that you will speak at the meeting.' There. When I come back I shall read those words and be either ashamed or elated.

But first, before I go, I must tend to a professional duty. During the last few days or so, perhaps even weeks or so, I have woefully neglected my students. How have they managed without my tutorials, my seminars, my lectures? Yes, re-establish myself as what I am, not mere Helena Twiscombe, but Helena Twiscombe prefixed by a Dr, terminated by a PhD. I shall begin by phoning the College office to uncancel all my cancelled classes, however many they may be. I can't remember exactly what excuse I gave, but probably I claimed to be the victim of a bug. There's generally some virus or another doing the rounds at College, not necessarily an intellectual one. There. A little joke. A little joke in the old Twiscombe mode. It cheers me up. So, to the telephone and – but of course the office will be closed at this hour. I glance at my watch. Good heavens, I must hurry if I'm to get to my meeting. I open the drawer and there is the gin bottle. It makes no impression on me whatsoever, no, none whatsoever, although it rolls about as if begging for attention, while I pull from underneath it the list on which I keep all my colleagues' phone numbers. I put the list on the desk, close the drawer emphatically, and run my finger down the column.

'Hello?' A young woman's voice. Bright and pretty-sounding. Most likely one of his students, at one of his 'informal' seminars.

'Hello. Is' – I remembered not to say Left-Overs or

68

Scruff – 'Dr Foster there?'

'No. No, he isn't, I'm afraid.'

'Would you be good enough to give him this message? Helena Twiscombe phoned to ask him to put a notice outside her door. Her seminars will proceed as scheduled.'

There was a pause.

'Have you got that?'

'Yes. But I can't, you see. Give him a message, I mean. He's dead, you see.'

'Dead? *Dead*? But – but how?'

'Suicide. He committed suicide.'

Now I mustn't pretend that I recall exactly how I replied to this – with bursts of exclamations, bewilderment, horror, I assume, but then what? Oh yes, an apology for intruding on her grief. Oh no, she said, that was all right, she was just the new tenant. Then she asked if I'd mind telling her something about Dr Foster. For instance, did he have a beard and wear those granny specs?

'Yes,' I said. 'He had a beard. And specs. Granny specs.'

'Oh,' she said. 'I keep seeing this, this, well, ghost, I think it is. Thin, with a beard. Like Christ. But with granny specs. Standing over my bed at night.'

I said that sounded like Dr Foster indeed, indeed it did. And then I said, 'Well,' I said, 'well, give him my regards when you next see him. Regards from Helena Twiscombe.'

Yes, I actually said that. I was desperate to stop the conversation, you see, get off the phone and report it back to myself, as I'm now doing, so I would know for sure it wasn't one of my hallucinations, another haunting. And it wasn't. I can still hear my voice passing on my regards to the ghost of a dead colleague and her gasp before I said goodbye and hung up. Whatever I feel for poor little Left-Overs, Foster, I mean, Foster! I must put aside, at least for now, hold on to what I'm doing. I shall phone, yes, yes, of course. Dialling. Ringing. Ah.

'Hello?' A familiar voice, rich and warm.

'Hello, Horatia,' I said, reassured. 'Helena here.'

'Ah, Helena, yes. How are you?'

I drew a breath. 'You know about poor little Left-Overs?'

'Who?'

'Foster, I mean, Foster.' I waited apprehensively. For quite a long time. Was I going to have to break the news?

'Yes, yes, I do. Very sad. Very sad indeed.' So that was a relief.

'We'll miss him very much.'

'Yes, yes. We do. We do miss him.'

'So do I. Already. Tragic. But Horatia, I wonder if you could do me a small favour? You're always at the College first thing, would you mind putting a notice on my door uncancelling my seminars, I'm completely over this bug, whatever it was.'

'Just a minute, Helena. Hang on a minute, will you?'

There was some whispering, muttering and whispering. Then another voice on the line.

'Helena? This is Esmé.'

'Esmé? But where's Horatia, I was talking to Horatia.'

Esmé's voice was thin. Thin and crawly with compassion.

'Helena,' it said. 'You really need to see someone.'

'See someone!' Did I bellow this? Yes, I think I did. 'What I really need is to talk to Horatia about a very simple matter. My seminars.'

'Helena, you haven't got any seminars. You were retired at the end of last term.'

'Retired? I was retired?'

'Because of your health. Helena. Helena, that's why,' still thin and crawly but urgent as well, 'that's why you need help. You see? Not only for your sake, but for other people's. This is the fourth time' – a mumble off – 'fifth time you've phoned Horatia in the last week or so. She gets very upset by it. We both do.'

'I'm sorry,' I said. 'Very sorry. It won't happen again.'

'That's what you said the last time.'

There was a long silence.

'Helena, are you there?'

'Yes.'

'Well, get help, Helena. Goodbye, Helena.' Click.

Let me think how I am. I'm befuddled, yes, but quite lucid in my befuddlement. To have forgotten so much! Is it possible that Sissy isn't even here? That all my forgotten time has been taken up with imaginings of her?

I've just come back from listening outside her door. Yes, she's here all right. I heard her voice on the telephone. I was so relieved that I nearly knocked on her door, called out, 'Ho, Sissy, there you are then.' But I didn't. Better not to see her until I've been to a meeting.

The secretary, a grey-haired man who introduced himself as Daniel, rather distinguished looking, with a majestic, even Roman profile – a retired bishop, perhaps, or ambassador – welcomed us with grave warmth, then, turning to the 'chair', introduced us to Denise, a crumpled woman in her early forties, actually she looked rather bedraggled, but bedraggled to a certain style, so possibly a social worker. It was a particular pleasure to him, personally, said Daniel, to have Denise in the chair this evening. He'd come to know her well over the years, had come to cherish her strength and kindness, her gift for communicating a kind of 'inner laughter', while maintaining a hard-earned independence of spirit. Yes, I thought, he's definitely of the clergy. Though I also had some idea I'd glimpsed him now and then on television, either in serious discussions on religious topics or in a popular television series, playing with dignity the role of senior surgeon, bishop or ambassador who turns out to be financially and sexually corrupt.

He gestured towards Denise, sat back, arms folded. Denise hunched herself, then crouched forward. 'Well,' she said, in a nasal, slipshod accent, 'Well yes, as yew just heerd from Dan, I'm what yew are stuck with for the next twenty minutes, yes, I'm Denise, I'm an alco'olic.' 'Hello, Denise', 'Hi, Denise', we hailed her.

I confess I didn't listen closely, fixing myself on the prospect of raising my hand in a request to speak. But fragments from Denise and her story, even though recounted with a dreary lack of emphasis, linger vividly. The drunken brawls in pubs, the time when a man smashed a telephone into the face of another man on her account, the black-outs, the waking up in strange rooms and gutters, the finding herself, on one occasion, at home in bed, two completely unknown women, one on either side of her, squabbling over which of them was entitled to 'first go', a problem she resolved by vomiting over both. There were further episodes along similar lines, which she punctuated by little glances at her watch. Twenty minutes was only twenty minutes, after all, interminable from one point of view (mine, so anxious to speak, so fearful of speaking) but brief from hers, as she had to cram in not only her degradation years but also the beginnings of her self-illumination, her first timid appearances at meetings, her battle for 'recovery', professional qualifications, a job. 'I mean,' she said, still crouched, 'I'm not claiming mush for mysel, only that I'm in tush wid mysel, and that's a fockin' relief, I can tell yew. And – and well,' as her eye caught her watch, the twentieth minute had come, was going, gone, 'thenyew for listen' to me, hope I haven' bin too borin'.' 'Thank you, Denise,' we said, 'thank you for sharing.'

The secretary Daniel then personally, most personally and graciously, thanked Denise for her 'exhilarating and rewarding chair', and threw the meeting open. My arm shot up. My nerve failed. My arm shot down. It must have looked as if I'd given a brisk Nazi salute. Someone else wagged his hand tentatively but with determination, got the nod from the secretary. His was a tale, soothingly told, of decline from prosperous businessman, loving family man to pub scrounger, draining the very last dregs of whisky, gin, vodka, cider, white wine, lager, etc., from glasses left uncollected on tables at the bar. Then stumbling around the litter-bins, unshaven, in tattered trousers, on to hospitals, failed therapies, followed by the slow, grim struggle back into the world through meetings, meetings, twice a day for years. And now, here he was, in 'recovery' at last, half-reconciled to his wife and children who'd moved to

Wales to get away from him, and whom he therefore couldn't visit very often, if he was to remain in employment as a shelf-stacker in a supermarket, but golly, by God! here he was, wasn't he? He thanked us for listening to him. We thanked him for sharing. As he sat down my right arm twitched into agitation, but my hand didn't move from my lap. So somebody else's hand, and so it went on, hand after hand leading into story after story, all of them similar, all details different. I sat there, acknowledging that I'd given away my only chance, letting myself be lapped by the misery and recovery of others. In a comfortable sloth. Yes, I gurgled, these are my people, I do indeed, indeed I do, 'share' with them. If only I had the courage – ah well, ah well, one day, tomorrow, at another meeting – what would surely be the last speaker, a floppy woman with sparkling eyes, a boutique-owning sort of woman, finished on a joke at her own expense that I didn't quite understand. As I, with the others, thanked her for sharing it, and the rest of her life with us, I stretched my arm up lazily. It was only when I saw the secretary's head nodding patiently, insistently, in my direction that I realized what I'd done.

'My name is Helena,' I said imperiously, 'and I'm an academic.' There was a little ripple of sympathy. 'I'm sorry. So sorry. I'll start again. My name is Helena,' I said at twice the volume, 'and I'm an alcoholic.'

'Hello, Helena', and 'Hi, Helena', they called to me.

I began by telling them a pack of lies. Well, not so much lies, really, as metaphors. So I told them a pack of metaphors, is perhaps the best way of putting it. But it didn't really matter, I thought, as I blustered along, what I said about poor Mumsy and Daddy. Being dead they would never know. Nor would my twin brother, who never existed, even before death, so why should he care? As for my real and living sister, she'll never know, will she, over there on the other side of the world, never know that here in London I was describing her to a public gathering as a helpless, sherry-sodden wreck who had to be confined to the small back room of her Australian bungalow for her own safety and the family's honour.

'Now for myself,' I said. 'Some years ago I realized that I was drinking far too much. I took professional advice' – I now recall, as I write this, that the advice was given to me, unrequested, by a college porter, who found me in my office in my usual midnight condition and had to assist me into a taxi – 'and started coming to meetings regularly until I believed that I had conquered the habit. Could take a drink now and then without fear of – of – without fear of returning to my previous unhappy condition. But look at me. My breath smells of gin. Many days and many nights of gin. My hands are trembling, my heart pounding, my stomach is livid. My bowels are loosening and tightening as if they're choking. Disgusting. Yes, I am disgusting to myself. Disgusting, disgusting!' I suspect that both of my last 'disgusting!'s came out as angry accusations, not of myself, but of everybody else in the room, particularly Daniel and Denise at whom I was glaring with inflamed and bulging cheeks.

Suddenly I was free. I spoke of my mortification, self-pity, the many years wasted, the boredom, oh, the boredom of the self unwanted, especially by me. On and on I went, mercilessly. I told them everything. The loss of my job, how and when I discovered it, the long memory gaps, the short memory gaps. All I left out was Sissy. I didn't want Sissy to be contaminated by my self-purification.

'Yes,' said Denise in the chair, 'Thenyew, Helena, for sharin' wid us.'

'Thank you, Helena,' from everyone else.

'Thank you, Helena,' said Daniel. 'I identify,' clearly making here a dignified leap of the imagination, 'with what you feel.'

So came the prayer of meditation, then the collection, then the tea, coffee, biscuits. I stood around, a cup in one hand, a cigarette in the other. A member asked me for a light. He was Greek, I suspect.

There. I've got it all down 'as it was'. Sissy still hasn't come to me. But I don't mind. I'm enjoying the waiting, almost savouring it, as I sit without a drink in my hand, without a cigarette between my fingers. Am I already on my way to 'recovery'?

As I wait patiently, unanxiously, I keep on writing. Let me think, let me think. Oh, yes, that time I stumbled accidentally into her bathroom, no, Helena, that won't do, I *knew* that she hadn't locked the door. Still, my intentions were entirely innocent. So why did that limerick pop into my head – Miss Twye soaping her breasts in the bath/Heard behind her a meaning laugh, and the dirty old man in the bathroom cupboard – is that how I looked to Sissy, as I stood gobbling apologies.

'It's all right, Hellie,' she'd said. 'I'm only in the bath, not on the loo.'

And yes, that's why I'd really come in. Not as a dirty old man coming for Miss Twye, but as Auntie Hellie looking for her niece from years ago, when she'd been

a child and I'd used her bath-times to educate her.
Readings of Lewis Carroll, then later Keats, then of
course later, when I was thinking of Chaucer and
Shakespeare, she'd outgrown the company of adults in
the bathroom.

Ah, there's her bedroom door opening. Movements
in the hall. Little grunts and groans. Almost pig-like.

The bottle is on the desk, close to the glass which is in
my hand. Under the desk, by my feet, is a carrier bag
containing two more bottles, which I'd purchased
between leaving the meeting and getting into my taxi.
Why didn't I write that down? Was it because I thought
it irrelevant? Irrelevant? That I bought two bottles of
gin immediately after the meeting. No, I bought them,
I used the phrase to myself at the time of purchase, 'just
in case'. How wise! What foresight, Helena! Because
'just in case' has turned out to be just the case. There
was a boil on the back of the driver's neck. It was like
the boil on my right buttock. If I were getting out of the
taxi now I'd probably lift my skirt, bend over, compare
our boils. It might cheer him up to know that there are
at least two of us with boils. Mine comes from sitting at
this desk for so long, his probably comes from all the
malignant eyes that fertilize the back of his neck. That's
why I sympathize with him. I, too, am being fertilized
by malignance, to my very bottom. The bottom of my
soul.

'Come in, my dear,' I called. Wolf to Riding Hood.

She stood at the door, her sturdy little legs planted
firmly, one hand in her jeans pocket, the other pluck-
ing the belt of her bum-bag. She may be short, Sissy,
but she's strong, athletic, from all her tennis, swim-
ming, hiking. In fact she looks just like me twenty-five

years ago, as I'd have been if I, too, had led the sporting life. Though my face wasn't such a perfect oval. And I had spots instead of freckles. And those eyes were never mine. Grey, slightly squinty eyes. And her mouth, I'd never had that mouth, which curves up a bit, generous and good-natured, her mother's mouth. Nor the hair of course. Lovely hair, that would flow all silky to her shoulders if she didn't keep it cropped. 'Why, why don't you let it grow and flow?' I say teasingly to her. 'I keep telling you, Auntie. Eric prefers it short. When he pats my head he can feel my scalp. He likes that.'

I sat looking at her, thinking of Eric's hand curled round her scalp, his fingers digging into it.

'Are you all right, Hellie?'

'Of course I'm all right, why?'

'It's just that you had that look. As if your tummy's playing up again.'

'No, no, tummy's fine,' I said, patting it. I just managed to hold down a burp. Then in spite of myself, belched. 'Well, a touch of wind.' As if it were howling away outside rather than howling up inside. 'Just settled into the chair. Prospect of work.' I gestured to the typewriter and the pile of 'in memoriam' filth beside it. 'An interesting insight into the female maleness of the males created by female novelists in the 19th century, Austen, Brontës, Eliot. Haven't seen you all day. Out and about a lot, I suppose.'

'Oh, just to buy a few pressies. And then the packing.' She waved to the various bundles behind her that I'd heard her pigging into the hall.

'You're going then? Off and away? Only just come and already gone?' It was a bark. I couldn't help it.

78

Her accent became twangier. Whiny.

'But that was always the arrangement, wasn't it? I mean, when I arrived I told you I'd be leaving this evening. Don't you remember?'

'Of course I do. What makes you think I don't?'

'Well, you sound almost angry, Hellie.'

'Sorry, my dear. Mind's somewhere else. Just sad that I've given you such short shrift.' What I was dealing with here was lies. Hers and mine.

'Oh, but that's why I love coming to stay with you. We each go our own way, it's so lovely and comfortable. Not like a hotel.' A fucking sight cheaper, too, I almost said but didn't. Instead:

'Have you been seeing somebody else?' I asked. Why?

'Seeing somebody *else*? What *do* you mean, Hellie?'

'Oh, a little London romance. These things do happen, I expect. When the cat's left at home the mouse will roam.'

She came a few feet into the room at last.

'Mouse?' She has her own sort of bark. Antipodean. 'Mouse!'

I barked the mouse aside. 'What time's your flight?'

'The taxi should be here in five minutes.' She looked coldly at the manly watch I'd given her on her twenty-first, crinkled her eyes, curved her lips. 'I used your account, hope you don't mind.'

I pounded my fist on my desk. 'Sissy, how dare you! How dare you even ask such a question! I told you to use my taxis whenever you want them! There was to be no discussion! I insisted on it! I insist on it!'

'Thorry, Auntie. And thank you.' She doesn't lisp often. Only when getting a lot for nothing.

'And what time do you get into – ?' I stopped myself from saying 'Thydney'.

'Oh, I don't know, Hellie. Whatever time the plane arrives, as Eric always says. You will make the wedding, won't you?' The prospect of ruining Eric's wedding to my Sissy was briefly enchanting. But from what I'd seen of him in photographs Eric would be urbanely Australian, as most Australians are these days. He'd mop up after me, 'Are you all right there, Dr Twiscombe, hey, Stan, help me get Dr Twiscombe out into the fresh air!' And then he'd nip back in, to give and receive his vows. Happy ever after until divorced, while I crawled about in the shrubbery ever after, bitten by insects, snakes, spiders. Vomiting and incontinent.

'I'll do my very best, my dear. But the wedding comes smack in the middle of term –' What term? Irrelevant. I thumped my knee, an agonizing blow as I'd forgotten that I still had the glass in my hand.

'Sissy, oh you silly Sissy,' I said, Sylvestering my knee. 'You're not going today. You're going this day week. It's here in my diary.' Not true. I may not know the unimportant facts of my life, whether I'm in employment or not, whether I'm sober or not, hallucinating or not, but I know everything about Sissy. I certainly don't need a diary to know the times of her arrivals, her departures.

'Oh no, Auntie Hellie, you've put it down wrong. I do the same all the time. It makes Eric furious, once I took him to the opera on the wrong week, to *Turandot* when it should have been *Don Carlos* the following week, but we managed to get some returns, so we got *Turandot* and *Don Carlos*, Eric was livid, he hates opera, he thought I'd done it on purpose.' Her eyes squinted frankness through this farrago of nonsense, though it was passingly agreeable to think of opera-hating Eric going through two operas in successive weeks. But it should have been the opera-loving Auntie Hellie who sat beside his Sissy. No, her Sissy. *My* Sissy.

'Tell me, Sissy. Tell me what you really did that night you didn't come to *Carmen*. I won't mind, my dear, whatever it was you did. I'd just love to know, that's all. To keep things straight between us.'

She looked alarmed. Really alarmed.

'Hellie,' she said. 'What do you mean? What can you mean? Neither of us went to the opera, because when I came back from the Sickert exhibition you were asleep at your desk with, with – well, with your glass and your –' she gestured to it.

'Well, that clears up that little mystery, doesn't it? Let me see your flight ticket, my dear.'

'But it's in my bum-bag, along with my passport and Australian money, I don't want to go sorting through –'

I held out my hand. She shook her head.

'I'm not showing you my ticket, Hellie,' she said simply. 'I'm not a child. And I'm not your child.'

No and no. How could she be, when I loved her so much?

'I was only trying to be helpful. That's all.' I stood up. 'You changed your ticket, didn't you?' I sat down.

'Yes, Hellie. I changed my ticket.'

'Is it my smoking? My drinking?'

'I don't see you drinking. You do it in here. As for smoking – Eric smokes, and I love, just love, being his passive smoker.'

'What is it, then, you want to get away from? I mean, I've always tried to make a home-from-home for you. I

81

look after your room when you're away –'

'I'm away eleven months a year, Hellie. Some years I don't come at all.'

'– nobody but you sleeps in that bed. Not since the first time you came. When I have overnight guests,' (what guests, overnight?) 'they have to doss down on the sofa in the sitting room. I always make sure your favourite food is stocked in the freezer, that Italian ice-cream, there are tins of the Heinz spaghetti you love so much –

'Not since I was twelve.'

'– there's a shelf of your diet Cokes, and boxes of that specially scented tissue that gives me an allergy.' This wasn't simple as she'd been simple, it was plainsong. Rhythmic, toneless, despairing.

She turned her head. 'Was that the bell?'

'No,' I said. Though it was.

'I'll go and see.'

'He can wait a few minutes. You've time.'

'Well, I'll go and tell him –'

'No, I'll tell him.' I came around the desk. Waddled powerfully around the desk – is that what she saw? Her Auntie Hellie waddling powerfully around the desk, straight at her. 'This is my flat. I do the bell-answering in my flat!'

'Oh, Auntie. Oh, Hellie.' She put her hand on my cheek. She wiped my tears off on the corduroy of her sleeve as she went down the hall, opened the door. A brief exchange, and then she was back, followed by the taxi driver, who removed her bags.

'He says we've got to get a move on. Because of the traffic.'

The alternatives swelled meaninglessly. They still do,

as I write this. I offered a cheek for a farewell kiss, held out my arms for a goodbye hug.

She trudged away from me down the hall, the little bounces of her bum-bag and knapsack my only farewells.

Now gone then. Gone to her happy-ever-after, until the inevitable divorce (I pray) and the years will pass, and she'll age, the crinkle become a wrinkle, the squinting, luminous eyes become opaque ('Hello, I'm Sissy, I'm an alcoholic.' 'Hi, Sissy.'), the buttocks, the breasts becoming the flabs of time. Then the loneliness, the developing waddle – or so I pray. But I'll never know, being long gone by then myself. She might live happily ever after, after all, with or without her Eric. I pray for that too.

I pour a very small gin, add another very small gin, and go on adding small gins until the glass is full. Light a cigarette.

And the good thing is that while I'm getting less and less sober, I'm also feeling less and less drunk. In a few minutes, when I've drained the glass, stubbed out the cigarette, I'll rise, go to the cupboard where I keep the chains. I shall swing one around the rafter in the kitchen, put a chair under it and make a padlocked loop for my neck. Then another chain for my wrists, padlock them behind my back, climb on to the chair, force my head through the loop, step off the chair. Or perhaps I shan't have to go to the kitchen. Perhaps I shall be found here at my desk, my hands clutching at the layers of fat behind which this unwanted heart – 'Later on, Sissy, my Sissy, my Siscombe,' I'll whisper in a few minutes, 'Before the setting of the sun, and the drawing down of the blinds, before the turning on of the lamps, I'll read Charlie D. to us.' Afterwards we'll have dinner. After dinner, bed. Sleep. Such a long, deep sleep we'll have as we fold gently into each other through the night. Nothing will disturb us. Not even the screams of the jets as they soar out of Heathrow, to Sydney, and such places, through the night.

0181
420
4088